DEADLY SEVEN

DEADLY SEVEN

7 Sinful Tales

Preston Dameron

For my mother.

Table of Contents

Intro by the Author

Lust, gluttony, greed, sloth, wrath, envy and pride. In the eyes of the Lord, we're all sinners. The problem is we don't admit to what sin we have.

For some people we deal with fantasies that don't take place at home. And keeping the secrets away from our significant others. Some would have problems when it comes to money, whether it's too much or not enough. To some people, too much is never enough.

What about instead of going to a fancy restaurant, you go into one of those cheap all you can eat joints. What if you're a fat, lazy slob who sits around doing nothing as your wife does everything. She'll get angry, and dump you for Raul the pool boy. Better yet, you're tired of looking at your neighbor cruising the streets in his new car. On the other hand, you're an arrogant fool who hates everybody or everything because of your selfish pride. If you answer each thought with a yes, there is a suggestion for you. WAKE UP!!

This isn't make-believe, this is real life, and we're dealt with a ton of garbage. You see it in the papers, on radio and TV, or the internet, or in the streets, and it's not good at all! As a writer, I write from my imagination. As a Christian, I write and speak from my heart.

These seven deadly tales are examples when dealing with sin, and to avoid the traps. The Bible said in Romans 3:23 that we have all sinned. I admit, I've sinned too. It also states in Romans 10:9-10 that when you find your faith in God, and in Jesus Christ you may be saved.

Ladies & Gentlemen, it's time for us to take a deadly field trip. I hope in the end, you'll be a little wiser when dealing with these traps in the long run. Let the journey begin.

Sin #1 LUST

We start our deadly sins journey with something erotic, something sexy, and something wicked. We start the tour with Lust.

We have various ways of dealing with this sin. One example would be like going to high school as a teenager, and imagine the head cheerleader walking down the hall wearing a bikini. On the other hand, for the women reading this, they think about spending time in a tropical paradise with a muscle-bound hunk.

We see images of lust in movies, on TV, on the web, in magazines. We see images hanging in our walls in posters or a calendar. Nevertheless, when you see the real picture, all you see is an illusion. What you're seeing is an image that feeds on somebody's ego. Whether it is a magazine, a calendar, or a catalog; we're seeing the same illusion. It's not good for the mind, or the soul.

Case in point; my first cautionary tale. It deals with a young model who's about to become the object to every man's desire. Yet, to one photographer he wants to have her all by himself. I call this tale:

THE EYES HAVE IT

The Eyes Have It
A tale of Lust

I n a studio apartment, a photographer develops a set of photos in his darkroom. The room is as red as a warm Carolina sunset. The photographer answered a phone call.

"Hello."

A sexy voice is on the other side of the phone. "Is this Ronn Edwards, the photographer?"

"That's me, how can I help you?"

"If you're not busy, could I set an appointment for a photo shoot? When is the right time to be there?"

Ronn is currently in a dry spell. "Anytime would be fine, right now I'm developing some pictures."

"I can be there in about twenty minutes if it's alright."

"That would be fine, I'll see you then. Bye-bye."

As Ronn hangs up the phone, he exits the darkroom. He gets ready for his new client. The photographer's job is to take a picture to look like a real life masterpiece the same way an artist works with paint. Ronn knows that everything needs to be perfect for his client.

With everything prepared, Ronn waits for his new client to show up. A fire engine red convertible arrives from out of nowhere. Ronn couldn't believe who stepped out of the car. The driver was hot, blonde, and beautiful. She wore tight blue jeans and a tight cut-off tank top displaying her toned body. Ronn stared at absolute perfection.

The driver introduces herself. "My name is Maryse; I called you for a photo shoot."

Ronn comes to his senses and greets his new client.

"Come in, the dressing room is to the right."

Maryse goes to the dressing room. Ronn didn't know who she was or where she came from, but he may have found his new muse. Maryse walked out of the dressing room in a slinky black dress. The dress fits her toned body. Ronn couldn't believe his eyes.

"You look beautiful, Maryse. Have you always looked this hot as you do now?"

Maryse smiled at Ronn's complement. "Thank you Ronn, I was a tomboy in high school."

"You can't be serious."

"I am. I was nerdy as a teenager."

Ronn could not accept what Maryse said. "You're kidding!"

"I grew into my looks during my junior year. I got asked out by almost every guy in school."

Ronn picked up his camera. "Okay, Maryse, I need to get a couple of headshots."

Ronn told Maryse to stand in the background for her headshots. Maryse has the looks to make it as a professional model. However, she has other things on her mind.

Ronn continues shooting pictures. "Is this photo shoot to help build your portfolio so you can present it to a modeling agency?"

"No."

"Are they for a Hollywood casting director?"

"No."

Ronn couldn't believe her response. "You've got to be kidding; I mean you're good looking. You're telling me this shoot is not for them."

"Nope, I'm doing this for fun. I mean you're only young once, right."

Ronn felt disappointed with Maryse's reply. "You're right, but to me; you look more like a natural. You should seriously consider being a model."

After Ronn took the first set of pictures, Maryse went back to the dressing room. Ronn's friend, Paul Furlong came in with a six-pack of beer and a large pizza.

"Hey Ronn, I hope you don't mind, but I brought some food over."

Ronn was getting hungry. "Thanks, Paul, sit down as I load some more film."

Paul looked over his shoulder at the hot sports car. "Tell me, who's the owner of the convertible?"

"That would be my new client. She's changing right this minute."

Paul wanted to stay for a while. "Mind if I observe, Ronn?"

"If you save me a few slices."

Maryse came out of the dressing room in a schoolgirl costume. Paul gazed at Maryse for the first time. He kept quiet and drank his beer slow.

Maryse looked at Ronn's friend. "Would you introduce me to your friend?"

Paul introduced himself to Maryse. "My name is Paul, I'm a friend of Ronn's."

Ronn offered Maryse some food. "We have a large pizza and some beer if you're hungry."

Maryse kindly objects. "No thank you, I don't drink. Do you have any water?"

"I have bottled water in the fridge."

Paul wanted to get Maryse a drink. "Allow me."

As Paul went to get Maryse her water, Ronn shoots more pictures of his model. Maryse kept thinking about Paul.

"Your friend is cute, Ronn."

"He's good for a few laughs too."

Ronn finished another roll of pictures. Maryse takes a quick break when Paul brought her water. Maryse took a sip from the bottle and heads back to the dressing room. Paul talked to Ronn about his new client.

"Ronn, do you think Maryse has a sexy sister?"

"If she did I would charge her double."

The two friends laughed, but Ronn thought his friend was seeing someone else.

"What about that cute Asian girl you're dating?"

Paul gave his friend a sad remark. "We broke up two weeks ago."

"What did she do, pour beer on your lap?"

"Not exactly, after we made love, she told me she joined the Air Force."

"She's in boot camp thinking of you right now."

Paul tells Ronn how he felt about the breakup. "Not if the note didn't say, 'I didn't please her in bed like her last boyfriend'."

Ronn felt Paul's pain, but a familiar voice got their attention.

"Oh, boys."

Ronn and Paul turned their heads and saw Maryse in a white cotton terrycloth robe. She heads to the backdrop, and revealed a red bikini underneath the robe. Both Ronn & Paul stare.

Maryse had to wait for her photographer. "Ronn, aren't you gonna take my picture?"

Ronn snaps out of the hypnotic trance and gets ready to shoot. Paul froze like a statue. Ronn couldn't believe what's wrong with his friend, especially when it's somebody he has just met. Maryse displayed her beautiful body as Ronn shoots from all angles. The photo shoot was a success, and Maryse felt like she hit a grand slam. Ronn knew he discovered a new diamond in a pile of coal.

After the photo shoot, Maryse got dressed to her regular clothes and thanked Ronn. However, Ronn worried about Paul, who still hasn't moved. Maryse heads toward Paul and woke him up with a kiss. Paul comes to his senses as he saw Maryse in her street clothes.

Paul came out of a rude awakening. "What happened?"

Maryse gave Paul an explanation. "You froze."

"I beg your pardon."

Ronn told his friend what happened. "When you saw Maryse in her bikini, you froze. Don't worry, she told me to make a couple pictures for you."

Paul said, "You did that for me, Maryse."

Maryse replied, "Hey, what are friends for."

Paul smiled with what Maryse had said. Ronn tells Maryse to stay while her photos developed. Maryse told Ronn she couldn't stay; she has some errands and will come back in a couple of days. Ronn couldn't help but want to try to figure out who she is, and he knew that Maryse's presence helped him a lot. Ronn struggled with his work, and the owner of the loft got on his nerves for the last few days with the rent. To Ronn, the appearance of Maryse today is like hitting the jackpot in the Ultra

Lotto. Ronn gets himself a beer and a slice of almost cold pizza. Paul gave his two cents about Ronn's new client.

"Maryse is the perfect woman, she reminds me of somebody I knew from school."

Ronn took a wild guess. "Was it the head cheerleader?"

Paul answered his friend's question. "No, it was Ms. Roberts, my biology teacher."

"Your biology teacher, Paul?"

"Of course, she can talk about DNA while having great T&A, if you know what I mean."

Paul's response made Ronn remembers. "I remembered Ms. Roberts, I pictured her in a go-go cage with 'sock it to me' painted on her body."

Both men laughed like crazy. They both have Maryse on their minds, but they both have different thoughts about her. Paul raised his beer can for a toast.

"Ronn, I propose a toast. To Maryse, who made both our dreams come true."

Ronn's beer can touched Paul's beer can. "I'll drink to that."

Both men ate the rest of the pizza and drank the rest of the beer. Ronn suggested that Paul sleeps in the couch while he goes to the darkroom and develop the pictures of his new model. As Ronn looks at the developed photos of Maryse, he asked himself who she is, and what strange power does she have over men. After they developed, Ronn hung the photos out to dry. Ronn headed off to bed.

Ronn goes to sleep, and he hears a voice telling him to wake up. He opened his eyes and saw Maryse in a silky red nightie.

"I'm not disturbing you, am I?"

Ronn got up and looked at Maryse as if he was dreaming.

"What are you doing here, Maryse?"

"I've come to see you, I thought about you all day."

Ronn had other thoughts in mind. "I thought you were thinking about Paul. You kissed him, remember?"

"I did, but I thought more about you."

Ronn couldn't believe what he heard. He wants to kiss the moist wet lips of Maryse, she disappears, and Ronn fell flat on his face. Paul headed to Ronn's bedroom as Ronn got up.

"Ronn, could you please keep it down, I've got a massive headache."

Ronn explained why Paul has a headache. "You're hungover. In fact, we're both hungover."

"Did you dream about Maryse?"

"I have, I dreamt she was in my room."

"Not as wild as mine, I dreamt she was a sexy genie."

Ronn was not in the mood to hear Paul's story. "Could you tell me in the morning? I suffered a rude awakening."

Paul felt disappointed. "Okay, could you tell me where the bathroom is?"

"It's also the dressing room."

Ronn turned on the lights and showed Paul where the bathroom was. Seconds later, Paul spent most of the night throwing up in the toilet.

***

The next morning, Ronn cleaned the dressing room the best he could. He also developed more pictures of Maryse. He hopes that Maryse would love her pictures showing how beautiful she is. Not to mention the ice blue eyes staring at attention. Unaware, somebody knocked at the door. Ronn turned off the red light to the darkroom to find out it was his boss from the modeling agency, Ms. Setzer.

"I hope I'm not disturbing you?"

Ronn closed the door. "No, not at all, I have a client dropping by."

"Do you mind if I look at them?"

"Not at all. While you're here, would you like something to drink?"

"I'll pass."

Ms. Setzer looks at Maryse's pictures. She's impressed with Maryse's natural beauty. "You know, Ronn, I made a deal with a new cosmetic company, and I'm looking for a fresh face."

Ms. Setzer looked at the pictures of Ronn's new client as Maryse arrived. Maryse got out of her car, and she brought a friend along. The two smiled as they enter the studio.

Ronn was happy to see his client. "Maryse, I'm glad you made it."

"I know the first thing I need to do was to see how good my pictures look."

Ronn saw Maryse's friend, who is as hot as she is.

"Tell me, who's your friend?"

Maryse's friend introduced herself to Ronn. "My name is Leyla. Maryse told me you're the best in town."

Ronn never consider himself as the best. "I'm lucky for the moment."

Ms. Setzer disagrees. "Lucky? I'm here to say that he's our best photographer in our company."

Ms. Setzer showed Leyla & Maryse the pictures Ronn took. Maryse was so pleased with the pictures; she decided to make another shoot. Ronn still has to spruce up the dressing room.

"I need to straighten up the dressing room, I'll be right back."

Ronn headed to the bathroom and in a flash, he cleaned up the remaining mess completely. A quick cleanup, a quick spray of air freshener and the bathroom is good as new. Maryse & Leyla both enter the dressing room as Ronn left.

As the models began to change, Ronn loaded up his camera. The girls came out in their slinky cocktail dresses. Ms. Setzer begins to see Ronn in action as he started takes pictures of the girls. After he took a couple headshots, Ronn goes to work. Both girls were having fun. Ronn wasn't sure why his clients are chuckling.

"What are you two giggling about?"

Maryse gave Ronn an explanation. "Leyla thinks you're cute."

Ms. Setzer begins to like what she sees, and Ronn is having a blast. Leyla wanted to spice things up even more.

"Do you mind if I take off my dress?"

Ronn laid down the law. "I'm sorry, Leyla. I don't do nude layouts."

Leyla couldn't believe that Ronn doesn't do layouts dealing with what he doesn't call art.

"I meant that I have another outfit to put on, I don't do any nude modeling either."

"Oh, that; sure go right ahead. I'll reload my camera for the next shoot."

Maryse & Leyla headed back to the dressing room as Ronn prepares to load another roll of film. Ms. Setzer studied Ronn's way of dealing with Leyla; she's pleased with Ronn's honesty. Leyla & Maryse had a pair of matching military costumes for their next shoot. Ronn stood at complete attention.

Maryse explained what the next shoot is for. "At ease, Ronn! We wanted to do something nice for Leyla's boyfriend."

"He's stationed in Hawaii for the last three months. I wanted to give him something to think about while he's there."

Ms. Setzer is in absolute astonishment for what Leyla had in mind. "That's wonderful, I'm happy that you're helping both our troops and your country."

Leyla gave Ronn a giant size American flag to use for the background. Maryse told Ronn there's going to be a big surprise in the end.

"I'll believe you girls when I see it."

Leyla makes sure with what her friend said. "You'll see it, and you'll believe it."

Ronn placed the large flag on the background for Maryse & Leyla's next shoot. Both girls were being all that they can be, as the shoot was getting good. The two models took off their uniforms to reveal their star-spangled bikinis. Ronn couldn't believe what was happening. Ms. Setzer couldn't believe what she has seen. After he finished the second roll, Ronn talked to Leyla about the photo shoot surprise.

"How in the world did you come up with the patriotic striptease?"

"I'm an exotic dancer; I work at the Golden Diamond. I wear costumes like the one you saw."

Ronn said, "I got one more round ready, get your costume ready."

Leyla heads to the dressing room where Maryse has already come out of wearing a silk robe. Leyla explained to Maryse why she was late, and that Ronn needs to talk to her.

"Leyla told me you talked to her about the last shoot."

"Yes I did, what do you do for a living?"

"I'm an aerobics instructor. Leyla is one of my clients, as well as my roommate."

Ronn wondered if Maryse knows about Leyla's job. "Do you know what she does?"

"Of course, silly. I wasn't thrilled at first, but when she made $600 on her first night. It helped a lot with the bills."

Ronn decided to ask Maryse the big question. "Do you have a boyfriend?"

"I don't have a boyfriend for the moment. I always get asked by guys at the gym."

Ronn froze after what Maryse has said. That was when Maryse told him she was between boyfriends. Leyla came in with a silk robe like Maryse's.

"I hope I'm not interrupting you two."

Ronn answered. "No, not at all. I was asking what Maryse does for a living."

"Oh, I'm ready for the next shoot."

"Let me get the bed ready."

Maryse & Leyla took off their robes to reveal sexy lingerie for the next shoot. The girls were having fun, especially when they took the pillows off the bed and started a pillow fight together. Ronn couldn't help but shoot pictures and called it a day.

When the shoot was over, Ronn talked to Ms. Setzer about the shoot. His boss is awestruck despite seeing the bed covered with feathers.

"You did well, Ronn. Messy, but well."

"Thank you, I'm sorry about the feathers."

Ms. Setzer thought there was no explanation. "That's alright, after the exciting photo shoot. I may have found my model for the cosmetic deal."

Leyla & Maryse changed back to their regular clothes and thanked Ronn for the photo shoot. Ms. Setzer wanted to talk to Maryse about some wonderful news.

Leyla asked Ronn what's going on. "Why does your boss want to talk to Maryse for?"

"I don't know, Leyla. She has something big in mind for her."

Ms. Setzer gave Maryse the great news, Maryse is happy with Ms. Setzer's decision. She told Leyla the big news. Leyla wasn't sure if she was happy for Maryse or if she's jealous. Yet, she's happy for Maryse getting the deal. Maryse gave Ronn a great big kiss on the lips. Ronn couldn't believe what happened; he almost stumbled after Maryse kissed him. Ms. Setzer asked Ronn if he was alright.

Ronn got a little flustered from the kiss. "I'm okay, a little shaken up."

Ms. Setzer took Ronn aside and has an important job for him.

"Ronn, since you took good pictures of Maryse. I wondered if you can do the photography campaign for Raveon Cosmetics."

Ronn was familiar with Raveon. "I've heard of them, aren't they the makers of that new perfume I saw on TV?"

"Nightshade."

"Sounds deadly."

Ms. Setzer agreed. "It sure is, but Maryse won't be the new face for Nightshade."

Ronn becomes concerned. "If she's not going to sell perfume, what is she going to sell?"

Ms. Setzer gave Ronn the obvious answer. "I guess with the way Maryse kissed you. She'll be selling lipstick."

Ronn noticed as he got lipstick on his lower lip. From what he saw in Maryse, he knew she was not like any other woman he photographed. What Ronn saw in her is a million dollar goldmine, and he wants to have a share of the profit.

Maryse thanked Ronn once again. "Ronn, thank you so much. Is there any way I could return the favor?"

Ronn thought of one idea. "Are you busy tonight?"

Maryse had to turn him down. "I teach a cardio boot camp class in about an hour and a belly buster class later on."

Ronn felt hurt, but Maryse tells him the good news.

"I am free tomorrow night. Would seven o'clock be alright?"

"I thought I would ask what time you want me to pick you up. Seven would be fine."

Maryse gave Ronn a kiss on the cheek. "I'll pick you up."

Maryse grabs her bag as she & Leyla went back home. Ms. Setzer left moments later. Ronn stood alone in his studio loft as if he was on cloud nine; it was grand.

***

The next day, Ronn got ready for his date with Maryse. After he groomed up; he saw the fire engine red convertible parked on the street. He leaves the studio apartment, and as the car opened; Ronn saw Maryse in a slinky, sexy, candy apple red cocktail dress.

Maryse smiles at her date. "Well hop in, hot stuff."

Ronn smiles and gets in the car. He's surprised how Maryse kept the car looking as it was brand new. Maryse bought the car three years ago, and she added a GPS and a new satellite radio system.

Ronn loved what he saw. "I love what you've done to the car."

"Thank you, I've had this car custom made since I first bought it."

"I thought the thing was brand new, especially the built in satellite radio."

Maryse was happy to hear about her car's new feature. "I had that installed last week. I always listen to the upbeat club songs. It's excellent for my aerobics classes."

"What type of music do you like to listen when you're on a date?"

Maryse shift the car on drive. "Let's say, I wanna rock!"

Maryse turned on the radio as she keeps her foot on the accelerator. Ronn looked in absolute disbelief. He couldn't believe what's going on as Maryse drove the hot red convertible like it was a drag race.

Ronn thought to himself, who is this woman, and what have I gotten myself into?

***

Moments later, Maryse drove her car into the hottest restaurant in town, Chez Chuy. Ronn looks at the place, and thought there's no way he could ever get in. Maryse made the reservations for the place. Once the two got in, they looked at the menu. Ronn had trouble understanding the words.

"What kind of language is this?"

Maryse understood the menu. "It's French."

"I don't understand a single word of French. When I eat, I speak through the drive thru window telling them to super-size my fries."

"That isn't a sign of healthy eating. As an aerobics instructor I try to teach the values of healthy eating to my clients."

Ronn thought his date is a major health nut. "Are you saying you're a vegetarian?"

"No, I eat chicken, fish and lots of fruits and vegetables."

Ronn wanted to know much about Maryse. "How did you get involved in the health & fitness industry?"

"I got involved when my father died of a heart attack when I was in high school."

"I'm sorry to hear about it."

"I loved my father. We use to fish; go to football and basketball games together. When I played girls' basketball, he went to all my games."

"How did you find out that he died?"

"I played at the state championship game my sophomore year when my coach told me about his death. I played my last game in memory of my father, and after that, I studied health."

After Maryse told Ronn her story, dinner has arrived. Yet Ronn was more concerned about Maryse as she cried. Maryse went to the powder room after telling her story. The waiter asked Ronn if anything was wrong with his date. Ronn tells him that she's alright; the truth is that he's worried about Maryse as well. And as Maryse came back to her table, Ronn acted like a gentleman as he gets the chair for her.

"I'm sorry that I was a little emotional, today is the anniversary of my father's death."

Maryse enjoyed her dinner. Ronn also ate his food. He wanted his dinner with Maryse to be more of a joyful event.

Maryse had one suggestion. "Do you feel like dancing, Ronn?"

"I'm not much of a dancer, I have two left feet."

"I'm in the mood to dance. Let's go to a nightclub and burn off this dinner."

Ronn couldn't believe this was happening to him. He's dating the girl of his dreams, and he has never been so lucky in all his life.

After dinner, the two drove off to the hottest nightclub in the city, the Inferno. Getting into the club was no problem for Maryse, because she knew the bouncer. She tells the bouncer that Ronn was with her, he let him in as well. As Ronn & Maryse enter the inferno, the music was loud, and the joint was jumping. Maryse was ready to boogie, but Ronn had no idea where this is going.

Maryse takes Ronn by his hand. "C'mon, Ronn, let's dance."

Ronn wasn't feeling like dancing. "I told you, I can't dance."

Maryse couldn't hear what Ronn was saying. She took Ronn by the hand and forced him to dance with her. As the two danced, the place was jumping. The music got so loud that no one can hear in the first place. Maryse didn't care; she wanted to be with a man she feels that she might be in love.

Ronn thought to himself as he looked at Maryse, who is this woman, and what power does she have over men?

After an hour of dancing, Maryse was ready for more fun. On the other hand, Ronn got tired. Maryse took Ronn back to his house, and the two kiss like crazy as they opened the door.

Maryse thanked her date. "Ronn, I had a great time. I hope we can do this again real soon."

"Why don't you stay with me for the night?"

"I have an aerobics class to teach, and I haven't brought any workout clothes."

Ronn is sad, but he understands. Maryse gave Ronn a great big kiss on the lips and went out the door as she says good night to Ronn. Ronn was so smitten with Maryse's kiss; he collapsed unto the couch and fell asleep.

***

The next couple of days were a little hectic for Ronn. After his hot date with Maryse, Ronn was having a dry spell. He called Ms. Setzer if there's any news about Maryse's cosmetic photo shoot. Ms. Setzer has no word on when the shoot takes place; Ronn begins to worry. Without warning, the telephone rang. Ronn picked it up.

"Hello."

The other voice on the phone wasn't who Ronn had planned.

It was Paul on the other line. "Hey, Ronn, I'm glad I called you."

"What do you want, Paul? I'm expecting a phone call."

Paul felt that Ronn was rude. "Not with that attitude, pal. I wondered if you want to do some guy stuff, the two of us."

"I could do that, I mean, work has been slow since Maryse got the cosmetic deal."

"Jeez, Ronn, it's not like you're dating her."

Ronn tells his friend what happened. "Well, I did go on a date with her."

Paul couldn't believe his own ears with what Ronn said. "You didn't!"

"I did. Please don't be mad at me, dude."

"I don't know whether to be happy for you or kill you. I'm happy that you're dating her."

"Thanks, man. I haven't heard from Maryse in a while."

Paul gave his friend advice. "Give it some time, bro. She'll call you in a while. In the meantime it's a guy's night out."

"Okay, you talked me into it."

"That's the spirit. I'll come over to pick you up."

"I'll see you then, Paul, bye-bye."

As Ronn got ready to wait for Paul, the phone rang again. Ronn thought it might be Maryse as he picked up the phone.

"Hello."

No answer

"Hello?"

There was still no answer, Ronn hangs up the phone with a disturbed look. Paul came into Ronn's apartment ready to go. Ronn asked his friend a quick question.

"Paul, did you call me a couple of minutes ago."

"No way, I don't even own a cell phone."

"Somebody called me and nobody answered. I don't know what's going on."

"Well don't stand like a sourpuss, let's go!"

And the two best friends went out the door. As they left, the phone rang, and the answering machine picked it up.

***

A few minutes later, the two friends head to the Golden Diamond. Ronn and Paul sat down and ordered a couple beers, and watched the girls dance on stage. Paul looked like a millionaire at a house of ill repute. Ronn thought of Maryse, and wondered if she called him not long ago. Paul hollered at almost every naked girl in the club. Ronn continued to stare at his beer. He didn't pay attention to a hot blonde in a sexy candy apple red dress asking if he wants a lap dance from her. Ronn turned her down. Paul worries about his best friend.

"Ronn, what is wrong with you, man?"

Ronn looked at his friend. "What are you talking about?"

"You had the hottest woman in the club come to our table. And when she asked you for a lap dance, you told her no!"

Ronn thought of ignoring Paul's rant, but he couldn't take the pressure of what Paul said. Ronn got ready to leave.

Paul wasn't done talking. "Dude, why did you turn her down?"

"I'm sorry, Paul. My mind was on something else."

"Are you sick or something?"

"No, I'm not feeling well."

Paul had trouble standing. "I wish I could take you home, but I'm afraid I'm drunk."

"I didn't drink, I'll take you home."

As Ronn tries to get Paul out of the club, a familiar face shows up. It was Leyla, and Ronn didn't expect to see her.

"Ronn, I didn't expect you coming here."

Ronn said as he was holding a drunken Paul. "It was his idea."

Leyla understood. "I trust you. I can tell by the hoots."

"Have you heard anything from Maryse?"

"I haven't heard from her since she got the cosmetic deal."

Ronn gave Leyla his card. "If you see her, tell her to call me."

"I will."

Leyla takes a pen and a napkin and gives Ronn her friend's work number.

"Try to call her from the health club."

"I will. Thanks."

Ronn looks at Paul feeling sick. "Okay, Paul, I'll get you to your car."

Ronn took Paul to his house in Paul's car. He later called a cab to take him back to his studio apartment. When Ronn got back to his apartment, he checked his phone if there was any messages. As soon as he found out there was no messages. He went back to the couch and goes to sleep.

***

The next day, the doorbell rang like crazy. Ronn woke up dazed; he opened the door to see Ms. Setzer standing at the door. Ronn invited her in.

Ms. Setzer becomes worried. "Are you alright, Ronn? You look like you were at a bar."

"I was, but I wasn't in the mood to drink."

Ms. Setzer sat down. "I've come down to talk to you about the cosmetics ads."

"I called Maryse about it for a couple of days."

"That is why I came here to talk to you, I've asked Raveon to hire you as the photographer."

Ronn felt the bad news was coming. "Are you telling me I'm not the photographer?"

Ms. Setzer couldn't face the truth to Ronn. She looked at Ronn feeling so hurt to admit what she had to say.

"I'm sorry, Ronn, they want somebody with a little more experience."

"Ms. Setzer," Ronn replied, "I've been doing photography for more than ten years. I discovered Maryse, I made her a star, and you're telling me I can't work with my star!"

Ms. Setzer tries to calm Ronn down. "Ronn, that's enough! I'm proud of what you did, but they made the stupid decision. I tried everything to get them to change their mind. I'm sorry."

Ms. Setzer asked Ronn if there's any way she can make him feel better.

"I want to be alone."

Ms. Setzer left, knowing Ronn wasn't happy with her decision. As Ronn goes to the refrigerator to get a beer, he heard the phone rang. He thought it might be Maryse. Or it could be the cosmetic company wanting Ronn do the photo campaign. Ronn didn't want to answer the phone. Instead, he let the answering machine get it.

"Hi, this is Ronn. I can't come to the phone right now, so please leave a message."

After the beep, a familiar voice left a message. "Ronn, this is Maryse. I need to talk to you..."

Ronn stood like a statue, ignoring Maryse's call.

"... I know you're at home..."

Maryse cried over the phone. "Ronn, I'm begging you, please answer the phone."

Ronn couldn't help but stay like a statue holding his beer. The phone rang again, this time it was Paul.

"Hey Ronn, its Paul, give me a call. I want to know if you're alright."

Ronn stood there like it was going in one ear and out the other. Ronn felt that he was the reason Maryse is now a star and his talent ignored. Maryse & Paul tried to help their friend over the phone, but he tossed them aside. Ronn drinks his beer until he drops his can to the floor. He then got down on his knees, and breaks down in tears asking God to help him.

***

Moments later, Maryse arrives at Ronn's apartment in her convertible. Paul later arrives in his truck. The two worry for Ronn's safety.

"Have you called him today, Paul?"

Paul nodded, "I tried, but all I got was his answering machine. I know he's in trouble."

"I called him too; I have the same problem you have."

Another car showed up. Ms. Setzer arrived to help Paul & Maryse.

Maryse noticed the driver. "Ms. Setzer, what are you doing here?"

"The same thing you two are doing, Ronn needs some help."

Maryse, Paul & Ms. Setzer headed to Ronn's studio apartment to make an intervention for him. But as they knocked on the door, there was silence. Ronn didn't answer back or open the door. Paul contacted Ronn through the intercom, but Ronn didn't respond. The three worry.

Paul thought of a simple response. "He's not home."

Ms. Setzer corrected him. "He is home; we've seen his car on the driveway."

Maryse takes a credit card from her purse and places it on the door lock. After she placed the credit card in, the door opened.

Paul looks in disbelief. "How in the world did you do that?"

Maryse looked at Paul with a sexy smile. "Next to diamonds, plastic is a girl's best friend."

The three friends go into Ronn's studio; as Paul turned on the lights, they saw something terrible. They saw Ronn hung himself in the middle of the room. The two women screamed in fear. Paul is in disarray to see his best friend commit suicide; he felt that Ronn's death was his fault.

He hugged Maryse and cry out. "Dear God, why couldn't I save him?"

"You had nothing to do with this, Paul. I'm responsible for Ronn's death."

Ms. Setzer knew they were innocent. "No, I'm the one who's to blame. If Ronn was the photographer for that campaign, none of this would have happened."

Paul made an agreeable suggestion. "We have to call the police. I'll get the body down."

As Maryse picks up the phone to call the police and an ambulance, the door seals them in. Ms. Setzer tried to open it, but it was no use.

"It's stuck! We can't get out!"

Without warning, Maryse smelled something funny.

"Does anybody smell smoke?"

Paul started smelling smoke as well, and figured where it came from.

"The smoke came from the darkroom, it's a deathtrap!"

The darkroom is on fire. The added fumes of photo developer made it difficult for the three to breathe.

Maryse screamed in fear. "We'll die of suffocation before we burn to a crisp!"

Paul saw a window and needs something to break it with to signal for help. He sees a dumbbell on the weight bench and picks the weight up to smash the window. A tennant headed to his car saw the window shatter; he called the police in no time.

As Paul gets rid of more glass from the broken window, the fire truck came to the rescue. They place a ladder up to the window and the fireman saw the victims inside. He first got Ms. Setzer out of the building, and then Paul escaped without any trouble. With two victims already out, Maryse was next to escape. The young model is afraid to get out as the deadly flames continue to rise. Maryse continues to scream, but the fireman knows what to do to save her life.

"Miss, stay calm, I'm going to get you out."

Maryse was in terror mode. "I can't! I don't want to die!"

The firefighter keeps his cool. "I won't let that happen. Now please, listen and stay calm."

Maryse walks toward the exit. She remained calm under pressure as the studio apartment continues to burn. The firefighter continues to help the young model out of danger.

"You're doing alright, miss. Now come up to the window nice and slow. It's okay, you're doing great."

Maryse reached the window, the fireman tells her to take his hand. She raised her hand; despite the fact she's trying to escape a fiery hell. As she takes the fireman's hand, and heads for freedom, she felt a tug on her left ankle. Maryse looked down and saw Ronn grab her leg.

"I'm... not... letting... go!"

Maryse is in the middle of a deadly game of tug-of-war between freedom and a burning death. In an attempt to save her life, Maryse takes her stiletto heel and attacks Ronn in the chest to break free. Ronn felt the pain, but continues holding on. The young model has her right leg free. And with all her might, she plunged the stiletto heel into Ronn's eye. Maryse escaped Ronn's deadly grasp, but the fireman couldn't hold on to her. As the fire went heavy, the fireman lost his grip, and Maryse was gone.

The fire department put out the fire, and Paul & Ms. Setzer waited until the fire was out. The two were sad by the tragic death of their friend.

Ms. Setzer begins to cry. "It's all my fault, Paul. I'm so ashamed."

Paul hugged her. "Ms. Setzer, Ronn brought all this on himself."

The fireman came up to tell them the bad news.

"I couldn't save her, the time we put out the fire, we only saw one burnt corpse."

Paul wished to see the remains. "I like to see the body, please."

The fireman took Paul and Ms. Setzer to the stretcher, with a body bag lying on top. As he opened the body bag, Ms. Setzer turned away from what she was about to see. The dead body had the charred remains of a red stiletto heel attached to his eye. Paul looked at the remains of Ronn. Paul asked the firefighter about the other person.

"What about Maryse?"

The fireman took off his hat, and gave more bad news. "When I tried to find her, there was no sign of her body."

Another fireman held an evidence bag that contains a remote control for the door. Paul couldn't believe his eyes. He looked at the parking lot and saw the fire engine red convertible vanished. Where Maryse has gone, nobody knows. She fooled everybody... almost everybody.

***

A few months passed since Maryse's disappearance. An old photograph of her in a bikini showed up in a magazine. Leyla looked at the magazine as if she missed an old friend. She headed toward the beach. She lies on the towel in a snow-white bikini, she sees somebody surfing towards the sand. Her long blonde hair reflected in the sunlight, her lean body has a radiant healthy glow. It was Maryse recuperating for two months after the fire. Leyla cheered her friend on.

"You got your confidence back."

"Thanks, I couldn't believe the nightmares from what Ronn did."

Maryse gave her friend some good advice. "I don't mean to be rude, but Ronn brought this on himself. You have nothing to do with his demise."

"But I still feel horrible."

Leyla has an idea. "I know a way to cure your problem. I talked to two great looking guys, and we're going out on a double date tonight."

Maryse looked at her friend in disbelief. "You're wicked."

The two ladies laughed, but loved the idea. However, since Maryse declares to be dead, Leyla asked her friend what she wants to call her. Maryse looked at her old bikini photo and knew what she wanted to call herself.

"Call me... Venus."

"Venus? That's a name for a goddess. It's perfect!"

The two ladies continue to laugh, but the name fits like a glove. As a teenager, Maryse wanted to be a goddess. And like the Roman goddess of love, she lived up to a certain premise. Goddesses aren't made, they're born.

Sin #2 GLUTTONY

Let's face it, we are what we eat; sometimes we like to eat too much. Whether its buffets, holiday meals, or eating contests, we have to eat.

However, the habit of continuous eating is not healthy for anybody. For example, every Fourth of July they have a hot dog eating contest at Coney Island and on that contest the competitors do not take a couple bites. In fact, they woof them down like crazy. Some people could eat about fifty or more hot dogs in a twelve-minute setting. If anybody has a reversal of fortune, by throwing up all those hot dogs; they would be sorry.

I'm not a dietician, but my advice to avoid the consequences of overeating is to slow down when you eat, and don't go for more than seconds. In addition, if you go into one of those "all you can eat" joints, take your time; they'll make more. Eat right, and eat smart.

For my next tale, it deals with a man at an eating contest of his own. The top prize is his life.

I call this tale:

THE DARE

The Dare
A Tale of Gluttony

In a neighborhood sports bar, a loud atmosphere surrounds the place. The kind of night where people gather watching the fights. Sometimes the folks would gather to observe a college football game that they couldn't see at home. Today it was different, they weren't here to see potential pros scoring a touchdown. They're not seeing two men beating each other up for a championship belt. This event deals with mass consumption; it was an eating contest.

Hundreds gather at Inferno's Bar & Grill to view the biggest chow-down event in town. The contestants chow down on hot buffalo wings with a mug of cold beer to wash it down. Some competitors took their time eating the wings along with drinking the beer. Others eat and drink like crazy until they get disqualified for regurgitation. The contestants ate wings like crazy, as the crowd counts down the final seconds. The air horn blasted a loud sound signaling that the contest was over. The judges look at each of the contestants' plates to see who ate the most wings. As the contestants drink their beer from their cups, the judges made the final decision. The manager of Inferno's made the announcement.

"May I have your attention please? The winner of the wing-eating contest is contestant #4!"

Contestant #4 jumped for joy. He collected his trophy along with a check for three hundred dollars as the crowd gave him an ovation. The manager asked who the person who won the event was. His name is Samuel Brendon. Sam's friends were cheering real loud as he heads to his table. His friends Brian Miller and Bill Krieger couldn't believe the excitement.

Brian gave Sam a handshake. "Alright, Sam! With the way you're going, you could compete at the national level."

Sam wasn't ready for the big time yet. "I doubt it, Brian. Those guys who compete have to go through intense training."

"You mean like the people at Coney Island on the 4th of July. I'll see you there in a couple of years."

Sam stood firm with his decision. "Brian, I said no. I almost hurl after the guy threw up next to me."

Bill also wanted to celebrate with his friends. "Sam, you did great, but you need to take it easy."

Sam had his way of celebrating. "Oh, I will, Bill. Once I have another beer."

Brian gave Sam some caution. "You won't be driving home for a while after sipping beer and eating those wings. Besides, nobody is going to believe what you did today."

"Brian, it was a simple eating contest."

Sam continued to drink his beer as a way of celebration. His friends become more concerned about him being a bad winner. All that Sam can do is celebrate for what he accomplished. For Sam Brendon, victory to him is sweet, but he didn't know that his victory would come with a heavy price.

***

The next morning, Sam woke up next to the toilet. After the contest, he thought of himself as a king, and the first thing that a king does is go to his throne. His throne turns out to be one of porcelain instead of wood. He dealt with the wrath from the eating contest. The smell from his toilet was so bad, anyone who lights a match within a ten-foot radius would be sorry. In a flash, the phone rang. Sam got up slow, and answers his cell phone.

"Hello," he answers in a weak voice, "oh, hi Brian."

Brian called Sam to ask how he was doing after last night.

"Quiet down, Brian. I have a hangover."

Brian already knew that, if Sam placed hot wings and cold beer in; sewage would come out. Brian asked Sam if he did not forget about the football game today.

"Ah, the game, I almost forgot. What time is it now?"

Brian tells Sam it was a quarter till ten, and he'll pick him up in fifteen minutes. Sam said he'd be ready. Sam heads to the shower.

***

A few minutes later, Brian drove down to Sam's house. Sam warned his friend not to blow his horn too loud.

Brian apologizes. "Sorry, Sam. I almost forgot you're still hungover."

Sam got in the truck. "I'll rest while you drive to the stadium."

"One piece of advice, Sam. Lay off the beer for a while."

"I couldn't agree with you more."

The two friends planned this get-together since Brian won the tickets from a radio contest. When Brian won the tickets, he ran a victory lap around the hospital, at the same time his wife gave birth to twins. In Brian's case, he got penalized for excessive celebration. As they arrived at the stadium parking lot, they set up for tailgating. Brian brought the grill as well as the ground beef and buns for the hamburgers. Once the coals started burning, Sam prepared the burgers for the grill. The two also saw Bill and his son, Scott coming in. Bill brought in an ice chest and a keg of cold beer. Sam cringed as he saw the keg.

Bill got the Rampager spirit. "Hey guys, ready for some fun or what?"

Sam still felt the effects from yesterday. "Bill, you picked a bad time to bring a keg."

Brian explained what Sam meant. "Sam recovered from the effects of the contest. Bringing a keg of beer only makes it worse."

Bill apologized. "I'm sorry, guys, I brought it for Brian and me. I also brought some sodas in the ice chest for Sam & Scott."

Sam couldn't believe what Bill did. "You brought your son to the game."

"Of course. My father took me to my first ball game, and I want to pass that tradition on to him."

Brian liked Bill's idea. "I salute you, Bill. I would like to pass that tradition along with my kids. If I had twin boys."

Bill gave Brian a nod. "What if your daughters are into sports?"

"Hey, what my wife doesn't know won't hurt her. I'll make sure to take them to the ballet, after I take them to the game."

The three men laughed along as Brian continued fixing the burgers. He asked Bill if Scott wants a burger once it's cooked.

"I'm afraid I brought some hot dogs for him, as well as brats for us, Brian."

"Hey, the more food, the merrier."

As Brian place the food on the grill, the smell filled the parking lot as the fans get ready for today's game. Bill's five-year-old son, Scott asked Sam a question.

"Why do people cook in the parking lot?"

Sam gave the young lad an explanation. "Because the food in the stadium is too expensive. Drinks can be even worse."

"How much do drinks cost?"

"Eight dollars for a beer and five bucks for a soda."

"What can I get for a dollar?"

"I don't think they sell juice boxes."

As game time approaches, the smell of barbecued food hit the parking lot. Fans were enjoying the aroma of burgers, hot dogs and brats from first time grillers. Veteran tailgaters enjoy ribs, chicken, and steak turning the parking lot into one massive picnic. Hoping the gates open for fans to see the action on the gridiron. Another group of tailgating enthusiasts enjoyed the pre-game ceremonies. One of them recognized Sam as he heads toward him.

"Well, well, well, if it isn't last night's big winner."

Sam saw the massive shadow behind him. "I'm sorry, but do I know you?"

The stranger introduces himself. "You better know me, you cheater. My name is Clyde Nolan; I was the four-time champion. I was going for win #5 until you came around."

Sam didn't want to pick a fight. "I'm sorry that I beat you yesterday, but my friends dared me to compete."

"Don't give me that excuse, 'Mr. My friends dare me to do this,'" said Clyde. "You stole at my shot of glory, and I'm here to get it back."

Brian tries to intervene, "Now listen here. We dared him to compete, and like you I'm surprised that Sam won, but holding a grudge doesn't help."

Clyde didn't like what Brian said. Despite the fact that he looked like a 600-pound gorilla. All the advice that Brian gave still couldn't calm Clyde down when he's about to snap Sam like a twig. However, a smell from Brian's grill turned Clyde from a mean ferocious lion into a gentle lamb.

"Wait one minute; I recognize that smell, those are bratwursts."

Brian started feeling relieved. "Of course, I'm fixing some right now if you're interested."

"Listen, I'll let it slide. I always love a good brat with mustard and sauerkraut."

"I'm afraid I don't have any sauerkraut. Could you take your brat with mustard and onions?"

"I have no objections. I'll be happy to return the favor one day."

"What are your friends fixing over there?"

Clyde finishes his brat. "We're fixing some barbecued chicken and baby back ribs. We'd be happy to have you over."

Sam didn't mind about Clyde's offer. "What do you guys think?"

Brian couldn't pass the offer. "Sure, why not. This is the first time we tailgated; could you give us some pointers?"

Clyde offered the olive branch. "I can arrange that. Drop by and get to know my friends."

Sam thought the confrontation between him and Clyde was going to be worse than a backyard brawl. Instead, they buried the hatchet over barbecue food outside a football stadium. Meanwhile, a radio station van, and a catering truck showed up promoting the tailgate before the start of the game. The road crew disc jockeys were there to get the noise from the crowd as game time fast approaches. The catering truck was there as a promotion made by the radio station. Kodiak Ben Lester, the radio station's DJ saw Sam's tailgate and wanted to talk to him.

"This is Kodiak Ben here at the Rampagers parking lot and everybody is getting ready for game time. I'm standing here with one of our fans. Tell me, young man, what is your name?"

"My name is Sam Brendon."

Kodiak thought he recognized him. "Wait one minute, I saw you last night."

"I don't think we met."

"Of course we have. I saw you at the wing-eating contest last night. I can't believe you won the contest, you must've had a lot of practice."

"No, I did that once, and I'm not doing it again."

Kodiak couldn't believe that Sam's win last night was a one-night thing. However, the goliath disc jockey had an ace up his sleeve.

"Gee, that's a shame, Sam. I thought you can keep your luck going for a chance to win Rampagers merchandise."

Sam wasn't sure what Kodiak has in store. "What do you have in mind? I can answer a few trivia questions."

"I don't think this is a game show, son. What I have in mind is a special type of contest."

The caterers brought a tray that's kept covered like a gourmet restaurant. Kodiak explained what he had for Sam with an evil grin.

"I've come up with a special hoagie that has about 3 pounds of deli meat and a pound of veggies on a one pound roll. Nobody has ever finished the whole thing. Whoever finished will win a Rampagers jersey, and one thousand dollars in cash."

Sam felt the temptation of taking Kodiak's challenge, and so does the rest of the crowd. Brian grabs Sam by the arm and tells him that it's not the right time. Clyde saw it as a way of getting redemption after losing the wing-eating contest.

"Hey! I like to give it a try!"

"Well, alright! We have a challenger! Who else would like to try my special sub?"

Brian objects to what Sam was going to do.

"Brian, I want to give this a try."

"Sam, believe me, I saw somebody try to do it."

"Did he succeed?"

"No, he was like the guys who threw up from yesterday's contest."

Bill wanted to throw his two cents in. "Believe him, Sam. I rather see you lose the challenge than lose your life."

Kodiak cuts in Sam's private pow-wow, "Last chance, Sam. I need to know if you'll do it."

Sam looked at his friends for a moment. Then he looks at Kodiak as if he sold him a used car with over a hundred thousand miles on the odometer. Sam heads towards his friends deciding to view this one. Kodiak is unhappy that Sam won't compete. Brian was glad to see Sam not taking the challenge.

"I'm sorry, Sam. It's for the best."

Sam refuses to give up. "Even though I'm setting this one out, I'm still interested in doing this."

"Trust me, Sam, and as a friend. Besides, I don't know what type of meat Kodiak has put in."

"Are you telling me the meat in the sub is mystery meat?"

"No, I saw someone try to copy the same ingredients you see in that sub. The only mystery is how in the world somebody like Kodiak would make that sub."

Bill added, "Not to mention if they would consume the whole thing in thirty minutes."

Sam couldn't believe it. "Thirty minutes to eat that behemoth? Is that all it takes to win the cash?"

Bill compared the sandwich to a big dinner. "Think of eating a thick steak with a two pound loaded baked potato on the side."

Sam got hungry with what Bill said. "To me that would be good eating."

Brian played the rude awakening. "And it would be a nasty belly ache for a couple of days. Add that sub to what we're eating right now; you would have a belly ache and a heart attack to match."

Sam took his friends' advice to heart. He believes that Kodiak's sub will be a challenge for him. If Sam succeeds, he wants to make Kodiak cough up more than a thousand dollars. He hopes that he do can what Clyde couldn't do, finish a sandwich that people may call, the Widowmaker.

***

A few hours later after watching a big win by the Rampagers, Sam & Brian headed home. They ate the leftovers from the tailgate. Sam ate his burger by himself as Brian looked at him. Brian knew that Sam felt disappointed for not taking on the challenge. He thought it was what is best for his friend after eating those wings from yesterday. Brian wanted to break the silent car ride between him and Sam.

"So, what do you think of the game, Sam."

"It was okay."

Brian didn't buy Sam's response. "Okay? The game was awesome! Scott was happy to get the game ball from that 3rd and goal in the 4th quarter."

"We're looking at a future MVP in Scott, Brian."

Brian knew Sam felt hurt by not taking on Kodiak Ben's monster sized-sub. As a physician, Brian knows the dangers of overeating. Not to mention the consequences from the fat and MSG from three pounds of cold cuts. The fat can clog Sam's arteries, causing him to have a stroke or a heart attack. On the other hand, Sam felt cheated by what he thought was pure destiny. Brian continues to drive to Sam's house. As they stopped there, Sam grabbed his food and thanked Brian for taking him to the game. Brian tells Sam something to cheer him up.

"Hey, Sam, we'll try to do something for the three of us to do."

"It won't be dealing with eating."

Brian thought of something better. "No, it would be dealing with something wild. Like going fishing off at Lake Melvin."

"Fishing, I haven't fished in years, and I need to get a license."

"It would be perfect, Sam. the three of us fishing and camping without the wives and kids."

A smile ran across Sam's face. "I love the idea. We need to get some time off to make it happen."

"Agreed, lay off the overeating for a while."

"Doctor's orders?"

"More like best friend's orders. Good night, Sam."

"Good night, Brian."

Sam heads to the house. He needed to be alone with the thought that turning down Kodiak's challenge had made him less of a man. He takes his food to the fridge and goes to bed early. Sam knew that the next time he sees Kodiak Ben in another radio locale; he will be ready to tame the untamable sub.

***

The next morning, Sam was jogging down the street. He kept thinking about turning down the opportunity to devour a sub that nobody conquered. It would be like the days of the Knights of the Round Table going to slay the dragon. Or a mountain climber risking life and limb to reach the top of Mount Everest. Sam thinks that accepting the challenge would be a great accomplishment, because he wanted to do it. As he jogs back to the house, he spotted Brian pushing the stroller with the twins inside. Sam couldn't believe his best friend is getting to be more of a hands on father to his daughters than a bro to him and Bill.

"Hey, Sam, I'm spending some time with the twins."

"I can see that. I'm getting my run in before I head to work."

"Safer than dealing with a five-pound sandwich."

"I don't know if I can work it all off if I succeed. Did you figure out what was on that sub?"

Brian got confused. "All I know is that the meat varies from time to time."

"Varies? What do you mean by that?"

Brian explains to his friend what Kodiak does with his sandwiches. "I have colleagues from the hospital who listen to Kodiak's radio show. Every time he makes one of those eating challenges, he would change the meat."

Sam understood what Brian meant. "You mean like the time he offered a trip to New York City a few months ago."

"With a five-pound Ruben."

"Geez, that's a lot of corned beef."

"Not to mention a pound of sauerkraut. The fat from that would plug up somebody's arteries."

Sam was in disgust. "I'm trying to get my heart in shape, and you're talking about heart attacks."

"I'm your doctor, Sam. I'm making it my business."

"I'm surprised you're not my psychologist."

Brian notices about Sam's behavior. "What do you mean a psychologist, Sam? Are you okay?"

"I'm alright, but I had a weird nightmare last night."

As Sam was getting ready to tell Brian about his bad dream, one of Brian's twins started getting a little cranky.

"Sam, could you tell me later tonight. I don't like to keep one of my princesses waiting."

"Sure, no problem. I'll take a shower and get ready for work. Take it easy."

Sam rushed off to his house as Brian takes the twins for a stroll. As he heads home for a quick shower before going to work, Sam's phone starts ringing. He decided to let the answering machine get it as he showers. After he got out, he pushed the play button. It turns out the phone call came from a cheapskate life insurance company.

The nerve of these people, he thought.

As Sam heads off to work, he drives downtown and sees a billboard for the world's largest hamburger. However, he thought that sign was too tempting. As he stops at the stop sign, he sees another billboard. This time it features a sexy blonde in a hot red bikini lying on top of a piece of cheesecake. Sam couldn't believe what he saw. All of a sudden, he heard a loud noise. It was the horn of an old pickup truck. Sam went his way as the guy in the truck shouted obscenities at him. Sam headed to work at the hardware store. He concentrated on his job sorting tools and mixing paint. He didn't focus on giant billboards, or anything dealing with food in general. In Sam's dream, every time he mixes and shakes up cans of paint, he imagines he is making thick milkshakes. Sam minded his own business when he saw a familiar face coming into the store. It was Clyde Nolan, in his construction gear.

"Well I'll be a monkey's uncle. I didn't know you work here."

Sam couldn't believe it either, he never expect Clyde would be his first customer for today.

"I've been working here for three years. It helped me through college."

Clyde couldn't believe what Sam said. "So you didn't go to college on an eating scholarship."

Sam laughed at Clyde's remark and gave him his reply.

"Not exactly, I didn't have any friends since I started high school. Once I entered college, I got to meet some good friends like the ones you've met at Sunday's tailgate."

"I went to college myself, Sam. I spent most of my time on the field turning quarterbacks into fertilizer."

"Played football, the Rampagers would've used you for a linebacker."

Clyde agreed, "I would've been the best, but all those dreams of winning championships went when I broke my knee."

"How did that happen?"

Clyde answered, "I was in a bowl game which was a dream for every college football player."

Sam would know the feeling. "I agree, you not only get the attention of the fans, but the possibility of playing for the pros."

"I wanted to play for my favorite team, The Los Angeles Demons. In one play, I tackled the running back, but when I blew my knee, the pain was unbearable. The doctors said there was a huge tear. They did surgery on it, but when next season came along; my knee wasn't the same as my body."

"That's horrible. I never thought linebackers would have it rough."

Clyde nodded. "I thought to myself what was I'm going to do. I couldn't provide for my family if I cannot turn pro. My father was a bricklayer for over twenty years. He helped build places like these. I thought that since my football career was over, God gave me an opportunity that I never know about."

Sam thought of what he learned from church. "The Bible says that when one door closes, another one opens."

Clyde gave a better answer. "More like he opened a window, and all I did was squeeze my butt through there."

Sam & Clyde started laughing at Clyde's remark. What he said to Sam was true to anyone dealing with problems that they couldn't handle by themselves. Sam decided to change subjects as he asked Clyde about Sunday's tailgate.

"How were you feeling since Sunday?"

"If you were talking about King Kong's specialty, I'm surprised I'm still alive."

"If it was the King Kong special, it wouldn't have any meat at all. Apes are vegetarians."

"I thought chimpanzees made that sandwich, not a 450-pound grizzly bear."

"I'm surprised it didn't have bologna or tongue."

Clyde looked at Sam in confusion.

"Now that's disgusting. Besides, I already had breakfast."

"Sorry, Clyde," said Sam as he was going to ask his customer something else. "I forgot to ask you if you want to buy something."

Clyde almost forgot why he came here. He had a list involving the only thing he needs.

"I need about eight of those 50-pound bags of cement; I'm working on a new building outside of town."

"What would the cement be for?"

Clyde gave an unlikely answer. "A health club, I mean with all the eating that we did in the last couple of days, we need to take better care of ourselves."

Clyde pats his big gut when he made the remark.

"You sound like my doctor."

"Was he the one cooking your food in the tailgate?"

"Yes he was. C'mon, let's get the cement."

Sam leaves the counter after Clyde paid for the heavy bags of cement. The two men head to the display of cement and Sam loads the heavy bags in a moving cart. Once all eight bags are laden, the two men go to Clyde's truck and load the heavy bags to the flatbed. Sam felt like he got more of a workout lifting those heavy bags.

Clyde looked at amazement. "Man, you handle those bags like they were groceries."

"It goes with the territory. Besides, you should see me handle heavy bags of mulch and potting soil."

"Thanks for the help, Sam. I hope we'll see each other again."

"I hope it will be with a couple of cold ones instead of eating a few hot ones."

Clyde laughed at what Sam said, but he knew Sam was right. The next time he thought of seeing Sam is when there are no challenges, or outrageous activities. Sam went back inside the store to carry on the rest of his day.

***

Meanwhile, as Sam got home, he heads off to bed. As he slept, he had a strange dream. In his dream, he was on the field of Rampager Stadium, and saw a chair and a table on the fifty-yard line. Sam heads to the field as he saw fifty thousand fans surrounding the arena cheering for him. Sam got confused with all the attention. On average, the attention would go to a Hall of Famer. A lone cheerleader escorts Sam to the table. As Sam sat down, he wasn't sure what was going on. All of a sudden, a voice appeared on the stadiums loud speakers.

"And now ladies & gentlemen, please welcome a man who would scare Goldilocks whenever he gets a chance. Kodiak Ben!"

Kodiak walks down to field with two hot girls, the crowd cheers at him like he was a rock star. Sam couldn't believe his own eyes. He thought that Brian, Bill, or even Clyde is pulling a practical joke. Sam becomes concerned.

"Alright, could someone please explain to me what is going on here!"

Kodiak plays the peacemaker. "Calm down, calm down. I'm here to give you a chance."

"A chance at what?"

"A chance for you to make history, Sam. I thought since you didn't accept my challenge at the parking lot. I decided to give you another chance."

"I don't like where this is going, I'm going home, right now."

Without warning, Brian, Bill and Clyde were there to cheer him on. Sam becomes more worried.

"Guys, what are you doing here!"

Brian gives his response. "We are here to encourage you, Sam."

"Are you crazy! As my doctor, you would never let me do something outrageous like this."

"Of course I told you that, but I want you to have some fun too."

"You never said that to me before."

Bill agreed with Brian. "Well now is the first time for everything."

37

"That's right," said Clyde as he picks up Sam like a small child and escorts him back to the table. As Clyde takes Sam back to his chair, Sam decides to give Kodiak a piece of his mind.

"Alright, mister. This has gone far enough. I don't know what kind of game you are playing, but I am going to end this right here and right now!"

Kodiak was a little more firm, "Sam, where is your sense of competition?"

"I lost it when I first came here. I want to go home. NOW!"

Clyde grabbed Sam by the shoulders and tells him he can't leave until he finishes his meal.

A lone cheerleader comes in and brings a cart over with Sam's special meal on a silver platter.

Sam thinks this joke has gone too far. "Is this your idea of a joke, Kodiak?"

"It's no joke, Sam. I made this sandwich for you."

The chair and the table that Sam sat at turned into a highchair. Sam couldn't escape as if he was like a one-year old.

"Let me go, right now or I will call the police!"

Kodiak becomes firm. "Well then, if you want to act like a baby. We're going to feed my special chicken salad sandwich to a chicken like you."

Sam's friends were laughing and cheering on as Kodiak force-feeds the sandwich to Sam. Sam was screaming as the sandwich was choking him making it uncomfortable to breathe.

"Eat every last bite like a good little boy."

Sam felt the sandwich left a bad taste in his mouth. Thus, he did the only thing a baby does when something is uncomfortable. He spat it out, right into the face of Kodiak.

"That is disgusting! How long was that mayo been out in the sun."

Kodiak was in an angry mood. He wanted make sure Sam finish the whole sandwich. In an abrupt moment, an unfamiliar sound came from Sam's stomach. He felt a sharp pain as if something was hurting him from the inside out. Brian removed the tray from the highchair and tries to examine his best friend. Sam lets loose a huge scream, as a live chicken came out of Sam's abdomen. Brian could not believe what happen. The crowd on the field screamed as they watched from the jumbotron. Without warning, broods of chickens were coming in as everybody ran for their lives. The chickens start pecking on Sam's body. As Sam screamed for the final time, he got up as feathers flew from a torn pillow. He turned on the light and cried as the violent nightmare of Samuel Brendon drew to a shocking end.

*****

A few days later, Sam Brendon kept a straight face after his violent nightmare. He acted like everyone else when somebody has a problem and tries to keep it a secret. Brian called him on the phone asking if he still wanted to go fishing, but Sam said no. Brian & Bill decided to go see their friend.

As they headed to Sam's house, they knocked on the door. Sam opened the door as his friends see him only in his pajamas.

Bill looked in concern. "Are you alright? You look like crap."

"I feel like crap, Bill. Come on in, guys."

Brian & Bill entered Sam's house, and they saw Sam's couch looked more like a bed. In fact, Sam slept on the couch for the last few days.

Brian shares Bill's concern. "Sam, what is wrong with you? You look like somebody came and stole your bed."

"My bed is still there, Brian. I haven't slept there for the last few days."

Sam's best friends sat down on the couch as he explains what happened. Bill start to worry.

"You look terrible, is it the same nightmare that you told Brian?"

"It's complicated," Sam replied. "The last dream I had was on the football field. You guys were cheering me on as Kodiak brings one of his sandwiches."

Sam continued telling his story to his friends. The two listened as Sam talked about his violent nightmare. Brian looked at his friend in concern.

"Jeez, Sam, that was a real nightmare. It reminds me of trying to get into the cool group at school. Everything you try to do is humiliating to somebody."

Bill shared his encouragement. "Sam, you are better than what Kodiak is dealing with, I dealt with guys who pledge fraternities in college.

They're the type of guys who drink beer and chase girls on campus. Kodiak is like those frat guys, nothing but bullies."

"You're right, and as long as he keeps playing mind games with me, he'll win. I don't want him to win."

Brian gave Sam a fair warning. "As your physician, I would have to be against what you would do. However, as your friend, I understand how you feel. I'm with you no matter what."

Bill grabs Sam's shoulder, and gives him a word of encouragement.

"That goes double for me. I'll admit that it was wrong for us to dare you in the wing-eating contest. When you see that big, bad, stinking, grizzly bear; you'll give him his just desserts."

Sam hugged his friends as if they were part of his family. Kodiak's tactics might be strong, but Sam, Brian & Bill have a bond that is solid. And those odds would never be unbreakable, or unbeatable.

***

A few days later; after he checked the radio station's website. Sam and his friends drove down to the parking lot of Rampagers Stadium. The encounter has come full circle for Samuel Brendon. Because to him, it was a second chance at redemption. Some came to the tailgate before the gates open, but Sam is waiting for a date with destiny. The same date with destiny that athletes look forward when a championship is on the line. Sam thinks facing Kodiak's challenge to him would be like a baseball player steps up to the plate. This time, he's got the bases loaded with one out remaining in the bottom of the ninth inning. And the home team is down by three. Sam knows that finishing whatever Kodiak made would be his grand slam. And if he fails, it would be like the Mighty Casey striking out, letting his friends and himself down. As Kodiak's van shows up, Sam talked with his friends about his last minute preparation.

Bill gave Sam the ultimate pep talk. "Do us one favor. Once you finish this, don't take any more dares."

"I'll keep that in mind."

Bill added, "Put the nightmare aside, or Kodiak will win."

Sam starts feeling confident. "Bill, today is bear hunting season. I'm going to hunt a Kodiak."

Kodiak comes out asking loyal Rampagers fans who wants to win money from him. He brought in a special five-pound sandwich that he called, the Bear. It's made of turkey, ham, salami, roast beef, lettuce, tomato, onions, pickles, mayonnaise, mustard, and Swiss cheese. All on a one-pound roll. Kodiak asked for volunteers.

"C'mon folks, who would be the one to take on the Bear?"

Sam looked at some of the people who would like take on the Bear. Instead, he confronted Kodiak himself. A big shock was on Kodiak's face.

"Sam, what are you doing here?"

"I accept your challenge. I'd like to take on the Bear."

Kodiak refused. "Forget it, buster, I gave you a chance a few weeks ago. You blew it."

Rampagers' fans booed on Kodiak's denial. Most of them chanted, 'Let him eat!' over and over getting Kodiak to act more like his namesake. Clyde Nolan was also chanting along with Brian & Bill. Kodiak had no choice but to let Sam compete.

"Okay, Sam. I'll let you compete."

The fans cheered for Kodiak's response for Sam to compete in the eating challenge. Kodiak explains the rules to Sam that he must finish the monster sandwich within thirty minutes. After that, he must hold it in for five minutes to win. Sam understood the rules. He goes to the table where the Bear is place in front of him. Sam prepares to feast on the enormous creation. Kodiak set one timer for thirty minutes while his radio colleague sat a second timer for five minutes. Kodiak asked Sam if he was ready. Sam gives Kodiak a nod as a way to say he's ready. Kodiak raised his arm up to fire the air horn as the eating contest between Sam Brendon and the Bear begins.

Sam starts by taking sensible bites instead of eating it ravenous like previous contestants. However, with a race between him and the clock, he needs to hurry in order for him to win. Sam's colleagues start to worry with the pace that Sam is going.

Clyde wondered why Sam didn't eat fast. "Why hasn't he chow down?"

Bill gave Clyde the reason why. "I don't think eating like an animal would be the right way to finish it. It's like drinking a whole bottle of hot sauce."

Bill added another example. "It's also like biting into a jalapeño without drinking a bottle of milk to wash it down."

Clyde becomes confused. "A bottle of milk. Why not a bottle of beer?"

Brian gave his best response as a doctor. "Because beer would make it worse."

"Jeez, I didn't know that."

Ten minutes have passed and Sam takes his time. He ate the first two pounds of the sandwich as hundreds of spectators cheer him on. Sam picks up the pace as he took medium-sized bites as Kodiak looks in shock. Sam continues eating as he finishes the third pound with fifteen minutes remain.

Brian cheers his friend on. "That's it, buddy. Keep the pace going; it's not time for beast mode yet."

With ten minutes to go and Sam ate four pounds of the Bear. Fans cheered as Sam eats slow with one pound of everything from the four basic food groups left. Five minutes left and a half a pound to go, Sam thinks that his stomach is getting the best of him. He was doing the best that he can do, but it feels like he was getting ready to stop much to Kodiak's chagrin. However, Brian gave Samuel Brendon a second wind.

"BEAST MODE!!!"

Sam goes on a feeding frenzy as he finished the Bear with only minute to spare. The whole crowd went bananas as Sam became the only one who conquered the unbeatable foe. Kodiak Ben had one more ace up his sleeve.

"Not so fast! Our eating champion has to hold the Bear in for five minutes in order for him to win."

The crowd booed at Kodiak in complete disgust. Clyde wanted to ball his hand into a fist wanting to turn Kodiak into an endangered species.

"C'mon, you creep! Sam won the contest fair and square. He deserves whatever prize you promise him!"

"I did promise him, he finished the first part. The other part is trying to hold it in for five minutes. So far, he has held it in for a minute and a half."

Sam continues to hold on after the second minute. The crowd cheers him on as the seconds wind down like a wild New Year's Eve party. Brian, Bill & Clyde were looking in as Sam continues to hold on.

Brian gave Sam some motivation. "Don't give up, Sam. Don't let the nightmare beat you."

Bill also cheer for Sam. "That's it, buddy. You're about to make history."

Clyde gave the biggest motivation of all. "The prize is all yours, Sam. Kodiak is going to lose."

With a minute to go, an attendant placed a trash bin in case Sam loses his lunch and dinner. The timekeeper keeps checking the time as everybody gets ready to count Sam down for the final seconds. The crowd started from ten as Sam held on to his stomach. After everybody shouted one, the sound of an air horn blared out. Samuel Brendon has made history from the parking lot of Rampagers Stadium. He has conquered the Bear. Kodiak stood in complete shock. He thought he made something that has defeated men and women who would challenge it. In the end, it only took one man to not only take the dare, but to conquer something that isn't conquered at all.

Kodiak knew that he was beat. "Congratulations, you are the first to beat the Bear. Do you have something to say to the people?"

Sam gave his only answer. "I have one thing to say to you. The next time you give away stuff from your station, try sticking to trivia questions."

"No kidding," Kodiak gave Sam his money, "you cost me a fortune."

Rampagers' fans cheered as Samuel Brendon conquered the Bear. Clyde, Brian & Bill were more amazed at what their friend did.

Bill cheered. "Way to go, Sam! I'm glad that you not only conquered the Bear, but your nightmare too."

Clyde nodded, "You are the best, and I respect you for that."

Brian gave one piece of advice. "I only have one thing for you to do, Sam."

"What will that be, Doc?"

"Start going on a diet. Doctor's orders."

"You don't have to tell me twice."

Samuel Brendon celebrated his personal victory over his nightmare. But like the wing-eating contest he entered a few days ago, he would deal with what he'll face later on; a simple bellyache. That's food for thought.

PRESTON DAMERON

Sin #3 GREED

Let's face it; we all want to be rich, it's human nature. Whether it's betting your life savings on a roulette wheel. Picking the winning horse at the racetrack. Or going for broke in an ordinary poker game; we like the easy way to make money. However, these choices are bad, and addictive.

Another conception of the classic get rich quick scheme is at your nearest store. Whether it's the scratch off kind or selecting the numbers for the big lotto drawings. Those games are from the state lottery, and it's seen throughout the nation. Only seven states don't have a state lottery. One of them is the state of Nevada, a place where gambling is king as well as sin. Some states even share big money type drawings by having a Multi-State drawing. They bring up big bucks and help for the states that sell them. The odds of winning them are at an infinitesimal high, and those odds are terrible.

What about the states that say the money used to help with our children's education? The truth is they don't give your children the education they need to stay successful.

In this writer's opinion, state lotteries and gambling are not the real solutions to be rich. Hard work, an educated mind, and a drive to succeed are the real steps to success. Those who win those jackpots had trouble keeping a low profile.

This tale that involves greed would also explain everything. It's about a man who's tired of making ends meet. When he wins the biggest jackpot in lottery history, he'll learn there are some things his money couldn't buy. I call this bizarre tale:

SIX NUMBERS TO RUIN

Six Numbers to Ruin
A Tale of Greed

All across America, there is a fever that's seen on every store. It spreads like a wildfire that won't stop until it's covered in black ash. It is lotto fever, and it's located everywhere. From a supermarket in Atlanta, to a gas station in Los Angeles. From a delicatessen in New York City, to a truck stop in Las Vegas. Everybody is playing the only lottery game that's played in all fifty states, the Ultra Lotto.

Unlike other lottery games, the Ultra Lotto placed 100 numbers in a huge drum until six numbers come out. If somebody has all six numbers on their ticket, then he or she will become a multi-millionaire. However, there are no cash prizes for people who match four or even five numbers.

Everybody would love to win the big ten billion dollar jackpot drawing tonight. Among those people is heading to a gas station to buy a potential winner. His name is Taylor Wallace, and every Friday he goes into a local gas station and orders a 12 pack of beer after work. However, when he heard about the jackpot is up to ten billion dollars, he thought he would give it a shot. He picks up the beer, and goes to the counter to pay for it.

Taylor went up to the cashier, "Could I have five dollars for tonight's Ultra Lotto drawing?"

The cashier rings him up. "Sure thing, are you looking forward to the big jackpot tonight?"

"I don't know, I'm not much of a gambler."

"I don't care much about the lottery anyway. Besides, the ones who say they're feeling lucky would later end up like suckers."

Taylor was not happy with the cashier's reply. He thinks there may be some people who do feel lucky, especially when big money is on the line. After Taylor purchased his beer and his lottery ticket, he drove back to his house. As Taylor heads home, he always thought of a warm welcome by his loving wife and family. However, every time he puts his car in the driveway, he always got the same old thing. He comes to the kitchen door with the twelve pack of beer under his arm. Tiffany Wallace, Taylor's wife of eight years, was not happy to see him.

"Where have you been? I'm almost finished making dinner, and you look like you're drunk."

Taylor retorted. "I don't drink when I drive. I stopped to not only get a beer, but to pick-up a soon to be winning lottery ticket."

"Aw, Taylor would you stop believing in that garbage. I know the Ultra Lotto is completely fixed, there's no way somebody can win by matching all 6 numbers."

Taylor thought he heard that talk before. "You sound like the cashier at the liquor store. When I win the ten billion dollars tonight, everything will be better for us."

"Better for us, don't you mean better for you."

"What is that supposed to mean, Tiffany?"

Tiffany knows exactly what Taylor had in mind. When she first met Taylor, he was a well-behaved gentleman. The two met on a Sunday during worship service at church. Taylor was nervous when he first saw Tiffany singing with the church choir. She had the voice of an angel, and he knew that she was the right girl for him. The couple started dating together since high school until they went to college. After a brief separation, the two reunited, and were soon married. Taylor worked in construction while Tiffany became a stay at home wife. However, there was grim news in the couple's future. The economy began to go down the tubes, and Taylor was off work for several months. The company calls him on a limited basis. Tiffany decided to try to find a job, which made things completely difficult. With ten billion at stake, Tiffany seems to be more skeptical.

"I'm saying that you're playing right into a trap, a trap that you can't escape."

Taylor looked into his wife's eyes. "I'm not hooked, baby; all I need is one good chance."

"Promise me one thing, baby."

"Name it."

"Promise me that you don't give your hopes up."

Taylor gave his wife a kiss as he gets ready for dinner. Tiffany feels sad; she wishes that Ultra Lotto fever doesn't consume her husband.

***

Hours later, Taylor Wallace sat down in his favorite chair waiting for the drawing to start. He picks up the remote control and turns it to channel 8; the Ultra Lotto was on the air. Everybody across the nation have their televisions set for the biggest jackpot in history. The host appeared with a sexy Vegas showgirl in each arm as he gets ready to draw the six numbers. Taylor grabbed a pencil and a piece of paper as the first number popped out of the machine. The host picks the ball up and calls it to the camera.

"The first number is 32."

Taylor writes down 32 as the second ball pops up.

The host receives the next ball. "The next number is, 59."

As Taylor writes down 59, the next number pops up; it was 10. With ten billion dollars at stake for one single winner, Taylor didn't pull any punches. The next number popped up revealing 95, and followed by 24. Taylor wrote each number as fast as he could. There was one number left to draw. That puts Taylor and the rest of the country left in suspense like an old serial cliffhanger. And as the last number is announce to the entire nation, the most horrible thing happened. The TV got cut off in the Wallace household. Taylor Wallace is completely devastated. He tried to get the TV back on, but the entire neighborhood is in a blackout. Taylor was mad, now he can't find out what the last number was. Not to mention seeing his dream of becoming a multi-billionaire goes up in a cloud of smoke. Taylor decides to sleep on the couch as Tiffany laughed to herself upstairs in bed.

***

Morning has broken, and everybody calmed down after the plague of Ultra Lotto fever. The paperboy tossed the morning paper right on Taylor's doorstep. Taylor got up after a serious hangover; after the blackout, he drowned his sorrows in a few beers. As he took off the rubber band, he read the front page, and discovered that two people won the Ultra Lotto jackpot. The numbers read 10, 19, 24, 32, 59, and 95. Taylor looked at his ticket and read each number from left to right. And as he looked at the ticket, he couldn't help but scream bloody murder.

"Yahoo! Thank you, sweet Jesus! I'm so freakin' rich!"

Upstairs, Tiffany thought the whole house was on fire. She ran downstairs to see her husband go berserk.

"What's with all the screaming!"

Taylor was in complete joy. "I did it! I did it! I won!"

Tiffany thought her husband lost it. "What do you mean, 'you won!'"

"The Ultra Lotto, my ticket matched last night's drawing, and I won."

"How can you win the jackpot? The whole town was in a blackout last night."

Taylor showed his wife the headline. "The numbers were in the morning paper, I looked at my ticket and all six of my numbers match. I won!"

Tiffany looks at the paper; she even looks at the ticket that her husband was holding. Tiffany could not believe her eyes.

"Do you know what this means, Tiffany?"

Tiffany knew what her husband is saying. "I know exactly what you're saying, Taylor. We're rich!"

Tiffany started jumping for joy. She wanted to get on the big multi-billionaire bandwagon right away. However, when Taylor saw his wife celebrating with him, he started to play the mine card.

"What do you mean, 'we're rich?' I bought the ticket with my own money, my ticket matched the numbers, and my ticket won the money. It's MINE!"

"But I'm as much as a multi-billionaire as you are, honey. Don't I deserve to be part of your success?"

"But you said the Ultra Lotto is completely fixed, you said I can't win."

"It IS completely fixed! Did you ever saw news reports on people who won a lot of money on those lotteries?"

"What about them?" Taylor asked in rhetorical fashion.

"The people who think that money would make their lives easier. In the end, their lives have been more miserable after winning the lottery."

Taylor wanted the win to be different. "Tiffany that is never going to happen."

Tiffany wasn't buying it. "Well tell me, Daddy Warbucks, what do I get from it? You remember when the preacher said for better or worse, and for richer or poorer. They're more than mere vows, they're promises that we made when we became husband and wife."

"Are you planning to cry me a river? You're doing a great job playing the wife card."

"I'm playing more than the wife card. I'm going to play my trump card. And if you don't include me or the kids in your success, I'll call a lawyer and I WILL take you to the cleaners."

Tiffany played her greedy husband like a violin. Taylor knows now that he either plays his wife's little game, or pay a lot of alimony and child support bills.

"You win," said Taylor. "I married you for better or worse, and I want to share my success with you for the better."

Tiffany hugged her husband and knows that she became what she wanted to be when she was a little girl. Her mom told her to marry someone who would take care of her. Taylor knows that he must find a way to keep the money for himself. And the only way to do that is to take care of the problem.

***

A few days after winning the Ultra Lotto jackpot, Taylor Wallace became the talk of the town. News of him becoming a multi-billionaire has been a shock and surprise to everyone who knows him. Some were happy to see him win the $5 billion dollar jackpot. Others thought about asking him for a couple thousand dollars. Taylor donated some of his winnings to the children's hospital and his church. He moved into a much better house and got himself and his wife a pair of brand new cars. Despite winning the lottery, Taylor hasn't changed at all. He's still the same miserable old self, but with a lot more money to make him even more miserable.

After all the prestige from winning the Ultra Lotto, Taylor Wallace can finally relax. He sits in his backyard enjoying the view and thought to himself, how the heck did he got there. His wife on the other hand is having a wonderful time, when she arrived with a handful of shopping bags. Taylor doesn't know if winning the Ultra Lotto is either a blessing or a curse.

"Whoa, Tiff, what did you do, buy out the store?"

"No, I'm getting ready for the party on Saturday."

"What party?"

"I thought since we won the Ultra Lotto, we wanted to do something nice for our friends."

Taylor decided to be more humble. "Since we won all that money, doesn't mean we have to show it off."

"I want it to be special."

Taylor looked at Tiffany and gave her a hug, and told her what they're doing now is special. It's hard for Taylor to be humble towards his family. His son asked him if he could have a swimming pool in the backyard. But Taylor tells him that he needs to learn how to swim first. What surprises Taylor is that nobody has claimed the rest of the jackpot. To him, somebody in America has a winning ticket, and not even know they have it. Without warning, the phone rang. Tiffany picked up the phone from the house.

"Hello."

The stranger on the phone said, "Is Taylor here?"

"Hold on, I'll get him."

Tiffany tells Taylor there was somebody on the phone. Taylor picks up the cordless phone and began talking. Tiffany heads to the house and overhears what her husband and the other caller were talking about. Tiffany eavesdrops on the conversation.

"How long will it take?"

The stranger gives him a modest answer. "I'll be in a couple of days for us to seal the deal. By then, you'll not only help us make more money, but you'll have more money than you know what to do with it."

"I'll look forward to it. I hope that my wife doesn't spend all my money before the deal starts."

The caller replied. "Taylor, you got nothing to worry about. It'll all be over soon."

Taylor becomes interested. "I'll see you at the party on Saturday. We'll discuss this when you get there. See you then, bye."

Tiffany hangs up the phone as soon as Taylor hangs up the cordless phone and goes back to the house. She tries to remain calm, cool and collected as her husband walks in to the room. Taylor gives his wife a kiss on the cheek as Tiffany plays along with what happened.

"Who was that on the phone, sweetie?"

Taylor explained who called him. "That was Ms. Ferris; she's going to be at the party on Saturday."

"What are you two going to talk about?"

"She and I are planning to go into business together. You'll get to meet her on Saturday."

Taylor goes to the living room with a can of beer. As Tiffany grabs her bags and heads to her room, she thinks there's more to the partnership than what it seems.

***

Saturday night, the time of the big party. It was a night for the Wallaces to give back to their friends. Some of their old friends arrive to celebrate the couple's new vast fortune. Taylor talks to some of his old construction buddies about their job. But as they continue talking, a stranger walks in looking for the young billionaire.

"Excuse me. I'm looking for Taylor Wallace, which one of you is him?"

Taylor introduces himself. "I'm Taylor Wallace, you must be..."

"Diana Ferris," she replied as she reached her hand out, "we talked on the phone a couple days ago."

"I didn't think you'd show up."

As Taylor's friends looked at Diana in suspicion, she asked Taylor a question.

"Is there any way we can talk alone?"

"Well, my study room is always quiet. We can talk about business, alone."

As Taylor head to the study, his friends could not believe what Diana looks like.

Benny was the first in denial. "Aw, man, Taylor is one lucky man."

Rocko couldn't believe his eyes. "Hubba, hubba. I need to win the Ultra Lotto."

Louie thought of a different topic. "I hope she has a hotter sister."

The other workers looked at Louie in disgust. Louie looked at them back in puzzlement.

"What! I mean if Taylor is with a hot dame like her. She must have a sister who is twice as hot."

Rocko gave Louie a reality check. "Louie, let's face it, you don't know a thing about women."

The rest of the crew walked out on Louie. Louie thought what he said was more of a compliment than a foolish remark.

Meanwhile, Taylor goes to the study to talk business with Diana. He needs to keep in mind about the risks and dangers on going to business with someone whom he hardly even knew.

"Let me get to the point, Ms. Ferris," he explains. "I'm a construction worker who in the last few months got lucky."

Diana wanted Taylor to relax. "It's alright, Mr. Wallace. I'm here to help you make more money."

Unbeknownst to Taylor and his soon to be business partner. Tiffany hid inside the closet in Taylor's study hearing the conversation.

Diana said, "When you invest in my company, I can make your financial dream a reality."

"First of all, Ms. Ferris, call me Taylor."

"Only if you call me, Diana."

Tiffany stays mum as she continues listening to hear her husband chuckle with Diana.

Taylor need time to think. "I need to talk to a lawyer about this. It's that I won the Ultra Lotto a few weeks ago..."

Diana interrupted, "Don't worry, Taylor. I won't let you rush things. All I wanted from you is a minute of your time."

Diana gives Taylor one of her business cards, and tells him to call her. She also gives Taylor a kiss on the lips much to the shock of Tiffany as she continues looking from inside the closet. Diana Ferris walked out of Taylor's study hoping that she sealed the deal. Taylor leaves Diana's business card on his desk as he leaves the study. As Taylor left, Tiffany comes out of the closet with a tear in her eye, and a heart completely broken. She gazed at the business card on Taylor's desk and memorizes the phone number. She dried her tears. As she leaves the study, Tiffany tried to look for Diana, and saw her leaving. And before she can stop Diana, Louie asked Tiffany where the bathroom is. Diana Ferris made a clean getaway, which made Tiffany Wallace, upset.

Moments later, the party was over, and Tiffany Wallace couldn't sleep as she cleans up the mess. She was still angry from what she saw that took place in her husband's study. Tiffany believes that nobody should mess with somebody's husband, especially her own. And the next time she would ever see Diana Ferris, it will be personal.

***

The next morning, the Wallace house was quiet, too quiet. After Tiffany Wallace cleaned the mess from last night's party, she slept on the kitchen table. The kids come downstairs getting ready for breakfast. Tiffany gets up, and fixes the kids homemade blueberry pancakes and sausage. Taylor goes downstairs and saw his lovely wife preparing breakfast for the family. As he tried to give his wife a kiss; Tiffany walked away as she fixes the food to Kelly & Justin. Taylor asked his wife where his breakfast is. His charming wife gives him a roll of sausage and a box of pancake mix and tells him to fix them himself.

Kelly asked. "Mommy, are you and daddy fighting?"

Tiffany didn't want to see the children get hurt. "No sweetie, we're not fighting."

Justin wasn't buying it. "But why are you telling daddy to fix his own breakfast?"

Tiffany tells the kids to take their breakfast to the dining room while she talks to their father. Justin wanted to see his parents argue, but Tiffany tells them to go without complaining.

Justin isn't happy. "Aw, man. I never get to see the good part."

Kelly didn't want to hear what her mom wanted to say to her father. And as the kids took their breakfast to the dining room, Tiffany was about to give Taylor a piece of her mind.

Taylor demands an explanation. "Why are you telling me to make my own breakfast? You know I can't cook!"

"Well cry me a river! I can't believe how you reacted to that tramp last night!"

"What do you mean by that!"

"I saw you kiss that bimbo in the study last night."

"How in the world did you saw me & Diana kissing?"

"I hid in your closet and saw you and your new business partner locking lips together."

"It's not what you think, honey. I was looking at ways to build a bigger income."

"You began to kiss a dream good-bye; A dream that we built on love and faith."

"I did not sell my soul to become a billionaire."

"No, but you bought in!"

"What do you mean, I bought in?"

Tiffany knew what she's talking about. "You bought in to the glitz, the glamour, the privilege of being rich. In other words, you bought into the hype!"

Taylor could not face the fact that the money he has won is now tearing his family and his marriage apart. He tries to think some way of how he would get his family back to love him. However, Tiffany tells him to leave her and the kids alone.

"I'm taking the kids with me to church. After that, I'm going to leave you, and I'm taking the kids with me."

Taylor looked to her in shock. "When are you coming back?"

"I don't know. I won't be coming back at all."

Tiffany walks out of the kitchen and tells the kids to get ready for church. As she leaves, Taylor sits down staring at a box of pancake mix and a roll of sausage, without knowing how to cook. He realized that he needs to think of what's more important, having a family who would love him even if he's not rich. Taylor needs to figure out what to decide before it's too late.

All of a sudden, the telephone starts ringing. Taylor answers it, and he figured out it was Diana Ferris on the other line.

"Yes Diana. No, I still haven't taken a look at the deal."

Diana tells Taylor that she is at the Starbright Motel, and tells him to meet her in twenty minutes. Taylor explains that Tiffany spotted them kissing last night. Diana asked if Tiffany was there.

"No, she took the kids to church. I'm here in the house alone."

Diana tells Taylor she's coming over; she wanted to finish what they started last night. Taylor thinks the visit is a bad idea, but Diana hangs up the phone, and gets ready to see her new client.

***

A few minutes later, Taylor saw Diana Ferris standing at the door wearing a mink coat.

"May I come in?"

Taylor thought it was a bad idea. "I can't let you in."

"It would only take a minute. I want to apologize to you and your wife."

"It's a little too late for that, please leave."

Taylor closes the door on Diana, not to mention their potential partnership. However, Diana doesn't give up. She noticed the garage door is open since Tiffany's car was gone. She goes in, and sees that Taylor went to the bathroom. As Taylor washed his hands, he heard a strange giggle coming from upstairs. Taylor goes upstairs to his room and sees Diana Ferris lying on his bed. She was wearing sexy red lingerie and white thigh high stockings. Taylor is now concerned.

"So, Taylor," said Diana with a smile of Judas on her lips. "Do you like what you see?"

Taylor gets mad. "You need to get out of my room and out of my house right now."

"But I can give you what Tiffany couldn't give you."

"I don't care, I will not have you destroy my marriage. And if you don't get out of my house, I will call the authorities."

As Taylor grabs Diana's mink coat and gets her to leave, a car headed back to the garage. Taylor knows whose car was coming in.

Diana starts to worry. "What is it, sugar?"

"It's my wife, she's coming back to get her clothes as well as the kids."

Diana asked in concern, "What should I do? I can't let her see me almost naked."

Taylor is in hot water, if his wife sees him with Diana then the marriage is over. He thought of something real fast.

"There's a room that is empty. I wanted it to be a nursery in case we want more children."

Diana ran to the vacant room, unaware that in saw her coming in. Justin turned to stone as he saw Diana for the first time. Tiffany comes up to check if he packed his bags.

"Justin, why aren't you packing?"

There was no response; in stood still. Tiffany snapped her fingers as Justin comes back to life.

"What's wrong, sweetie?"

Justin told his mom what happened. "I saw a woman with no clothes on going through that door."

Tiffany gives in a hug. "Mommy will take care of her, honey. Get your bags packed, okay."

As Justin goes to his room to start packing, Tiffany heads to the empty room. She opens the door and saw an open window thinking that Diana escaped. Tiffany leaves the room unaware that Diana hid in the closet and attempts another escape. She opens the door thinking the coast was clear. She leaves the room and this time, she's the one who's surprised.

"You scared me, sugar. Could you help me get out of here?"

Justin started to act smart. "I'm sorry, but I don't talk to strangers, lady."

Diana begins to lose her nerve on a little kid's remark; she offers Justin a bribe.

"Please, kid, help me find a way out of here. I'll give you toys and candy. C'mon what do you say?"

As Justin gives Diana his answer, a familiar voice gives an answer for him.

"Leave my son alone!"

It was Tiffany, and she was getting ready to give Diana a piece of her mind. But Diana goes downstairs and got into her car like a crazed maniac. As Tiffany regains her sanity, she goes to Justin to see if he's alright.

"Are you okay, sweetie? Did the lady hurt you?"

Justin told his mom how he feel. "I'm fine, mommy. She scared me."

"Well, mommy's here, sweetie. You finish packing your bags while I go have a long talk with daddy."

Tiffany kisses her son on his forehead and sends him to his room. Tiffany confronts Taylor, and gives him a piece of her mind.

"You're not gonna let it be water under the bridge!"

"What do you mean by that?"

"There was a woman running around our house in her underwear. What's worse is that our son saw her."

"I tried to get Diana to leave."

"Well it's too late. You had her hiding in that closet hoping that I wouldn't wring her neck!"

"I didn't make a move on her, she made a move on me. Believe me when I say this, I tried to get her to leave. I'm not doing any business with Diana Ferris."

Tiffany felt hurt. "I do believe you Taylor, but I don't trust you. You chose the money over your family. I don't know how to say this, but I'm leaving."

Tiffany takes off the wedding band ending her marriage.

"I set you free, Taylor. I hope you have a better life."

Taylor looked at the ring on his right hand that his wife wore for eight years of marriage. He stood still as Tiffany takes the kids and leaves him for good. A single tear falls down from his face, and lands on his hand touching Tiffany's ring. Taylor Wallace knew that all the money he won from the Ultra Lotto could not buy the love he once had for his family.

As Tiffany drove off with the children, she couldn't help that she missed being rich. Kelly and Justin missed the part of having what they always wanted. Tiffany started crying; unaware that her daughter spotted the tears on her face.

Kelly wondered why her mom is sad. "Are you alright, mommy?"

Tiffany holds back. "I'm fine, angel. Mommy's been dealing with your father."

Justin didn't like the long trip. "Will we see daddy again?"

"I don't know, honey. The only thing I need now is a miracle."

As the children sat quiet in the back seat, Tiffany saw a piece of paper that fell on the floor. When she stopped the car, she ignored it. Tiffany kept going all the way to her mother's house. As the kids got out of the car, Tiffany grabbed the briefcase as she spotted the piece of paper. As she picked it up; she noticed the numbers were 10-19-24-32-59 and 95. They were the same numbers that her husband played when he won the Ultra Lotto a couple weeks ago. In fact, she bought the same ticket the time the jackpot was around ten billion dollars. Tiffany Wallace smiled as it was a huge blessing from God. A teardrop fell down on her face, as it was a tear of joy. Justin looks at his mother standing in the driveway, and goes to ask her a question.

"Are you okay, mommy?"

Tiffany looked at her son. "I'm fine, sweetie."

As Tiffany gives her little boy a hug and a kiss, she gives the suitcase to Justin and tells him to head inside. As she settles down, she decided to contact the lottery office and explains her side of the story.

***

A few days later, Taylor Wallace sat down watching the news. He saw a report that made him cringe. He heard that the lost winning ticket is also won by his estranged wife, Tiffany. Taylor's jaw dropped as his wine glass hit the floor, and shatters to pieces. Taylor couldn't believe he felt betrayed for having his wife leave him. But sneaking out of the house to get a lottery ticket without notice. He figured out where she's living for the moment, but he already knew where she is. As Taylor gets ready to leave, he stepped on the broken wine glass and shouted obscenities. Taylor sat on the floor to remove the piece of broken glass. As he removes the glass, he bandaged up his foot. Taylor heads to where Tiffany left to get answers.

***

When Tiffany Wallace was a little girl, she thought somebody would marry her and make all her dreams come true. She never thought that when she left the lap of luxury that Taylor provided. Now she finds herself back in the lifestyle because of a lottery ticket she forgot. She stayed with her parents as she looks for a house of her own. As she looked in the classified section of the newspaper, her mom looked at her as if she needs help.

"Tiffany, it's getting late, dear. You should get to bed."

Tiffany couldn't concentrate. "I'm sorry, mom. I was checking at some houses to move."

"Can't you do that first thing in the morning? You need to get the kids to school, and they don't want to see their mom asleep at the wheel."

Tiffany understood what her mom said. Out of the blue, she had something on her mind.

"I need to ask you a question."

"What is it?"

"Have you or daddy been unfaithful to one another?"

"Heavens, no. Although there were times I wanted to knock your father out with a cast iron skillet."

"What do you mean by that?"

"When your father was about Taylor's age, I have a cast iron skillet. And when your father goes out playing poker, he comes back smelling like cheap cigars and stale beer. So if he try to make a pass at me, I try to hit him over the head with a cast iron skillet."

"Did you ever hit daddy?"

Mrs. Wilson giggled. "No, dearie. Every time I took a swing at him, he ducks down and hits the floor."

"It's hard when Sunday morning comes around."

"It did, but when God opened your father's eyes one Sunday, he became the man I once remembered before he married me."

"I wish that Taylor would be the same person I knew before the Ultra Lotto. However, you know what they say, 'money is the root of all evil.'"

Her mom touched her shoulder. "No, it's how we handle money. The only thing evil was in your husband's mind."

As the two ladies continue their conversation, a car comes in to the Wilson place ruining their front yard. It was Taylor Wallace, drunk and with a gun in his hand. Mr. Wilson looked through the window and tries to lock the front door. He tells Tiffany to keep an eye on the children, Tiffany rushes upstairs to make sure they're okay.

Kelly starts becoming afraid. "What's going on, mommy? Is that daddy coming in?"

Tiffany makes sure her kids are safe. "Yes, its daddy, but he's not coming in this house."

Justin worries about his father. "Is he going to be alright?"

"He'll be fine, baby. Mommy's going to talk to daddy, I need you two to stay upstairs and be quiet."

The kids hide upstairs as Tiffany goes downstairs to confront her estranged husband. When she went to the kitchen, she saw her father out cold from the door he tried to keep Taylor out. She saw Taylor with the gun on her mother shouting obscenities to her asking where Tiffany is at.

Mrs. Wilson becomes petrified. "Taylor, how could you do this at my home!"

"Shut up, you old hag!" Taylor demanded. "I want to talk to your good for nothing daughter right now!"

Tiffany stands up for herself. She couldn't let Taylor be on a killing spree filled with drunken rage.

"Leave my family alone! It's me you want, and I'm right here!"

Taylor was glad to see his wife safe and sound. "Sweetheart, thank God you're safe. I've come to take you and the children home."

"Don't you call me, sweetheart? You tried to come here with a gun trying to kill me and my family, and you've been drinking earlier. That makes you a danger not only to us, but also yourself."

"C'mon, Tiff. I need you!"

Tiffany saw through the lies. "What you want is the other half of the money."

Taylor starts to get mad. "You heartless witch! You have what's mine, and I demand you give me the money, now!"

"I'm not giving you one cent for threatening me. If you want my money, you would have to kill me."

As Taylor points the gun at Tiffany, he heard the sound of police sirens surrounding the Wilson house. Taylor gets mad over the arrival of the sheriff's department at the front door.

"You shameful hussy, you called the police on me!"

"I didn't call the police. I do think you need help, and the money you won made you less of a man."

"It's too bad this has to end this way. You and me would have it all."

Taylor cocks the gun and gets ready to pull the trigger. And before he gets ready to shoot, there was a loud clang to Taylor's skull. And as Taylor starts falling down, he fires the gun and the bullet hits the cookie jar. Tiffany opened her eyes to see her mom holding the cast iron skillet like a tennis racquet.

Tiffany Wallace breathes a sigh of relief as the deputies enter the house. They arrested Taylor on the spot and charged him with assault, DWI, and attempted murder. Tiffany sees her two children downstairs and rushes in to hug them. Justin told his mom that he & Kelly went to their grandparents' bedroom and called the police. Tiffany kissed both of her children telling them they have done well. Mr. Wilson had a bump on his head, but he'll make a full recovery. Tiffany Wallace won't worry about the greedy husband who almost took her life and her money. She can now finally start over to raise her children and living her own life.

Meanwhile, Taylor Wallace was guilty of trespassing, DWI, assault and battery, and attempted murder. He serves a sentence of fifteen years in prison. During mail call, he received divorce papers from Tiffany saying that she's taking the kids and leaving him forever. The news was devastating for Taylor, when he took his own life the following day.

Taylor Wallace once had it all, a loving wife, two caring children, and a troubled career. But when he won the Ultra Lotto, he thought his money problems were over. Instead, he head towards a wrong path, a path that leads to greed. And if somebody travels on a path of greed, the path will not go on route to Easy Street. Greed can lead someone like Taylor, to a quick way on the road to riches. And whosoever follows the greedy road will find himself facing a dead end.

Sin #4 SLOTH

For this sin, this is common for some people, even as I am writing this right now. We all feel bored in life with nothing better to do. I often feel the same way. The problem we have for sloth called procrastination. Putting things off because we tell them that we're too busy. We always put it on the back burner for the last possible moment. Some examples include doing our homework, cleaning the whole house, or spending time with that special someone. We are always too lazy.

In Romans 12:11, Paul tells us to "never be lazy, but work hard and serve the Lord enthusiastically." My question to you is, what would happen if Jesus would knock on your door, and you tell him no. Saying I'll do it tomorrow. I have news for you; tomorrow will be too late. If you die without making Jesus your Lord and keeping God first in your life, the consequences will be deadly. So please, don't put off tomorrow what you can do today. Because what I'm saying is more truth than fiction.

Somebody needs to tell the person in my next tale about what I said. It's about a slacker who has a chance encounter with a wake-up call. I call it:

THE LIFE CHANGER

The Life Changer
A Tale of Sloth

A cloud of smoke surrounds a small bedroom. The smoke was not as thick as a San Francisco fog, but you have to cut it with a knife to go through it. A stereo played over the room. The sound of loud rock n roll music and the mixture of the smoke filled the room as if it was a trip back to Woodstock. However, it was not 1969; this is what's going on today.

As the smoke gets heavy and the music got louder, a next-door neighbor comes to the door to complain. Mr. Kowalski shouted a rant laced in profanity like he wanted to get a battering ram and knock the door down from its hinges.

"I know you're in there, mister. I smell smoke, turn off that loud music or you'll be sorry."

As Kowalski continues knocking on the door with almost every obscene word he said. Jason Edison, the person who lives in the smoke filled room stood up and turned down the stereo. He also heard the loud rant from his neighbor. Jason goes to the front door, opens it and confronts his neighbor.

"What is your problem!"

Kowalski gave his explanation. "Every time you kept playing that music, it's been giving me migraines."

Kowalski smelled the smoke from the room and he knows that it didn't come from a cigarette.

"Not to mention that smoke coming from your bedroom smells like a college dorm. This crap has to go. I swear that if you continue doing this, I will take action and call the police."

"Whatever."

"Is that all you can say, 'whatever?' When I'm through with you, you won't be saying a word, period!"

As Kowalski left, Jason turned the stereo back on and goes back to smoking pot. The neighbors feel like Jason was rubber and everyone else is glue. Kowalski was not fooling; he was serious with the trouble Jason caused since he first moved in. Jason was once a good student in college until he spends his days partying in the frat house. His grades were slipping and got kicked out of school. Now Jason is on his own, and causing trouble in his quiet apartment complex.

As Jason continues smoking pot, drinking beer, and listening to loud rock n roll music. He heard another knock at the door, but it was Officer Norville telling Jason to turn it off completely. The officer started smelling smoke from the marijuana, enough to place Jason Edison under arrest.

***

Jason spent two nights at the county jail for drug possession, and disturbing the peace. Unaware to Jason, someone paid off the secure bond. Jason couldn't believe who paid off his bail. He knew that it couldn't be his folks because they disown Jason. He also thought it was his girlfriend. He thinks that she had a soft spot for him even though she thought he would drop dead. Jason asked the officer who has paid for his bond. The officer looked at the bond and there was only an X on the signature.

"There is no signature on the bond, son. Whoever did that wishes to remain anonymous."

Jason left the country jail worrying who paid for his bail. Why was he given a second chance at life when everyone else ever thought he existed? As Jason heads to his apartment, he didn't hear the complaints of other neighbors. He did not hear the cries from the small children. Jason opens the door, seeing that nothing changed from the arrest. After a refreshing shower, he decided to go to bed and wants to put the nightmare behind him.

***

The next morning, Jason Edison smelled smoke. The smoke didn't come from the cigarette made from the leaves of a cannabis plant. The smell came from his kitchen. Jason came in with a hockey stick in his hands getting ready to find out who is in his house.

The stranger is happy to see Jason was awake. "Oh, you're up. Good."

The stranger fixed a plate of bacon & eggs for Jason. He tells Jason to have a seat as he makes a plate for himself. Jason couldn't believe that this stranger would come to make him breakfast. Jason thought that something isn't right. Out of the blue, the toast popped out of the toaster. The stranger grabbed the toast, places a pat of butter and a smear of grape jelly, and gives it to Jason.

"I took the precaution of buying the groceries."

Jason slides the plate back to the stranger and gives a stern look.

"Look mister, I don't know who you are or where you come from; but you don't come into my house and fix me breakfast."

The stranger looks at Jason and gives him this reply.

"Shut up and eat your breakfast before it gets cold. NOW!"

Jason couldn't believe his eyes. The stranger pours himself a cup of coffee from the carafe, and offers Jason a cup. Jason poured himself one and as he took a sip, he notices that something isn't right.

"What kind of coffee is this?"

"French vanilla roast."

Jason spat the coffee back to the cup and put it aside. He started to get angry.

"Are you trying to poison me!"

"No, you've already done that yourself," said the stranger. "Lying down on the couch smoking cannabis and listening to loud rock music. Making the neighbors complain like an angry mob."

"Whoa," Jason gets up from his chair. "Who are you and why are you invading my privacy and my house?"

"Oh, where are my manners. I forgot to introduce myself to you."

The stranger hands Jason his business card. The card read:

LAWRENCE H. TILLMAN IV
Life changer Extraordinaire

"Life changer?"

"That's right, Mr. Edison. I'm here to change the way you've been living the last couple of years."

"That's a bunch of bull, Mr. Life Changer. You don't know a thing about me."

"I don't have to read your mind to find out your girlfriend dumped you."

"She never cared about me."

Tillman disagreed. "On the contrary, she cared a lot about you. I also know your parents worry about you when you were in college."

"That is not my problem, the reason why I wanted to stay in campus was to get away from my parents. They always keep making things difficult for me."

"That's why you drank at a younger age. Why you were smoking pot at times. Newsflash, Jason. This is not the 70s, this is real life, and I'm here to make sure you'll change your ways, or else."

"I'll show you what 'or else' means to me."

Jason grabs Mr. Tillman by his jacket and sends him towards the door and out of his apartment.

"AND STAY OUT!"

As Jason locks the door to his apartment, he turned around and got a rude awakening.

"That was not nice, Jason."

Jason looked in confusion as he saw Tillman back in his apartment. He opened the door and noticed that Tillman was not outside his door. A smile ran across Tillman's face.

"I told you, Jason, you're not getting rid of me."

Jason becomes confused. "How did you come into my apartment without a key?"

Tillman gives a twisted smile. "Let's say, I have my own ways of helping you."

"Who sent you to help me? I didn't need any help when I got sent to the clink."

"I'm here to help you, Jason. The least you can do is thank me for paying your bail."

Jason starts to laugh. "You paid for my bail. Don't get me started; I rather spend more time in jail to wait for my hearing."

His Life Changer was more serious. "I've seen what our prisons look like, Mr. Edison. It's overcrowded as is. And like our Lord and Savior paid the price for the sins of our world. I paid for the sins you have done for the last twenty-one years. In laymen's terms, you owe me big time."

"What I do with my life is none of your business!"

Tillman disagreed. "That's too bad for you, Jason. I'm making your life my business."

"I don't need your help. I didn't want your help in the beginning, and I sure as heck don't want your help right now."

"You will need my help."

"No, I don't."

"Yes, you do."

The two kept arguing like spoiled children until there was a knock on the door. It was Mr. Kowalski, and he was angrier than ever.

"What's the big idea, Edison! It's not enough for you spending time in jail, now you're getting to be noisy without having your stereo on!"

"I don't have my stereo on, Mr. Kowalski. I was talking to someone."

As he looks for Mr. Tillman, he vanished. Jason couldn't believe his own eyes. He had to make an explanation and fast.

"I'm sorry, I was arguing with myself. It won't happen again."

Kowalski becomes sterner. "For your sake, kid. I hope not."

As Jason closes the door, he heard an unfamiliar voice.

"You're skating on thin ice, son."

Jason thought he had a heart attack when he saw Tillman appeared in his couch.

"I'm surprised he didn't use your intestines for a jump rope."

Jason wanted to kill his new life coach. "You could've helped me, you idiot. I wanted to introduce you to that tub of lard."

Tillman stood up and gave the only explanation for why he didn't interfere.

"I forgot to tell you, you're the only one who could see me."

Jason laughed at Tillman's remark. He thought it was one big joke.

Tillman became serious. "I am not joking, Mr. Edison. You are the only person who can see me."

Jason sat down on the couch with what Tillman said. He believes all the drinking and drugs he did have caught up to him like a pit bull biting him in the butt.

"Who do you think you are, something from my imagination?"

Tillman gave his logical answer. "No, and you're not five-years old."

"Am I smoking too much pot?"

"No, it is not from the pot you smoked. I'm here to help you, and yelling at me has solved nothing."

Jason is not convinced with Tillman's remark. He started to pull the drawer from the end table, and grabs a sample of his emergency stash. Jason gives a firm statement to his new life coach.

"Let me get this straight. If you came here to help me, and you're not a figment of my imagination. Then I'm gonna roll up my emergency pot, and smoke this right in front of you."

Tillman gave his client a warning. "I wouldn't do that, Jason."

"You are not my father. You're not the boss of me."

"No, but you're released from jail for smoking that garbage in the first place. If you smoke that again, then you'll go to jail again. I won't be around to save you."

"You're bluffing."

"No, I'm serious. You are dealing with a weak hand."

"I say you're full of it, Mr. Life Changer Extraordinaire. I'm about to make my call."

As Jason placed the rolled-up roach on his lips and gets ready to light it. Tillman gives a gesture turning the roach into a real cockroach. Jason couldn't believe his own eyes as he spat out the cockroach from his mouth in disgust. Tillman grabbed the cockroach from the ground and made it disappear.

Jason was sick to his stomach. "What the heck did you do!"

"I'm going to change your life for the better, Jason. We can do this the easy way, or the hard way. The rest is up to you."

"I can think of another way we can do it."

"And what way is that, Mr. Edison?"

Jason answered. "No way!"

"No way?"

"Yeah, there's no way I am going to let some sissy guardian angel reject change my life. I guarantee that when you're gone, I'll continue to do what I want, and you can't stop me. Do I make myself clear, Mr. Life Changer?"

Tillman call Jason's bluff. "You've made your point, Jason. However, I'd check your end table if I were you."

Jason looks at his end table to see his emergency dope surrounded by a den of snakes. Jason jumped back at what Tillman had done.

"Do you think this is funny!"

"From what I saw, I find it hysterical."

"How did these snakes got in my end table?"

"What snakes?"

Jason looked at the open drawer and found the snakes have disappeared.

"Where do they go?"

"What do you mean?"

"What have you done with the snakes? Not to mention my stash?"

Tillman gave a devilish smile. "They're both gone. My first act as your life changer is making you quit your vices cold turkey."

"Cold turkey?" Jason gazed at the empty end table. "Have you lost your mind?"

"No, you are," Tillman had one more ace up his sleeve. "There's also one more way we're going to do things around here. My way."

Jason disagreed. "I rather deal with the snakes on the end table."

Jason walks toward the fridge and grabs a can of beer, but as the beer would go to his lips; he was in for quite a shock.

"What happened to my beer? This is nothing but water."

"Nothing gets by you, doesn't it?"

"At least I have my music," said Jason as he heads to his stereo. Unaware that instead of loud heavy metal music, he hears the heavenly sound of a church choir. Jason had enough.

"Alright, Mr. Life Changer, this crap ends right now! First, you took away my stash, and put poisonous snakes in the drawer. Then you replaced my beer with water. Finally, you replaced my heavy metal albums with a church choir singing a song that sucks more than a vacuum cleaner. This is all your fault!"

Tillman doesn't think so. "All my fault, Mr. Edison? Have you looked at yourself in the mirror lately?"

"What is that supposed to mean, Dorkasaurus Rex?"

"It means Mr. Edison that you are living in a fantasy world. You keep blaming everybody but yourself."

The two men continue their argument back and forth like a tennis match. Jason decided to end this squabble once and for all.

"I'm gonna go to the bar. At least I'll be happy."

As Jason gets ready to leave his apartment, he heard a series of beeps in the room. Jason thought that his new life coach installed an airport metal detector at the front of his door. Instead, the noises came from Jason's ankle. It was a house arrest ankle bracelet. Lawrence H. Tillman IV has done it again.

"I'm sorry, but it seems that you and I have other plans."

Jason is furious. "You did this, you put this little tattletaler without me knowing. Why are you doing this to me?"

"You know why, Jason. All you do is slack off, and I'm here to keep you busy. I recommend that you get a mop, and a bucket, and get this house cleaned up."

Jason laughed at the way Tillman was acting more of a mom than a life changer.

"What is so funny?"

"You are the biggest dorkasaurus I have ever met. You're a lot worse than my mom."

Tillman stood firm. "This pigsty isn't gonna clean itself, Jason. My suggestion is for you stop slacking and start cleaning."

Jason is mad; it's hard enough for him to spend time in jail. Now he's dealing with somebody who got on his nerves.

"Forget it, I'm going to bed. I've already been in jail, and now you're turning my apartment into San Quentin. I hope you are gone when I wake up from this nightmare."

"I'll still be around, and so will the mop and bucket."

"You won't be when I'm through with you. You can't treat me like a three-year old."

"Well then, quit acting like a child, and start acting like a grown-up. Then I'll be out of your hair."

Tillman gives Jason a mop and a bucket, and gives his troubled client a stern command.

"But right now, I want you to start cleaning this apartment, right now."

Jason had no choice but to follow Tillman's orders. During the rest of the day, he cleaned the house by himself. Tillman sat on the couch drinking his afternoon tea and reading the financial papers. Jason was furious seeing Tillman slacking off while he's doing all the work.

"Would it hurt for you to do your so-called Christian duty and help me."

Tillman ignored Jason as he continues cleaning the apartment. Tillman monitors Jason like a hawk going after small prey. He felt that in order for Jason Edison to break down, he would do more than make him do simple things. Tillman believes that Jason is more like a walnut with a hard shell to crack. Jason cursed up a storm to himself. As he cleaned the house, he wanted to grab Tillman by his neck and wring it. Jason felt that he's embarrassed by the tasks that Tillman is making him do while he's getting all the breaks. Jason imagines Tillman doing all his work while he smokes a bowl and listens to his music real loud.

As Jason finished cleaning the apartment, he locks the door and lies in his bed. He wanted to get away from Tillman's schemes and doesn't want to hear the name Lawrence H. Tillman ever again. However, as Jason slept in his room, there was a knock on the door. Jason wouldn't answer. All of a sudden, the knocks become louder, and the young slacker wants Tillman out of his life.

"Go away, Tillman!"

The knocks continue to get louder.

"I said, leave me alone!"

Tillman continue to knock on Jason's bedroom door louder and louder.

"If you want to talk to me, Tillman. You have to break the door down!"

Without warning, the loud knocking stopped. Jason went back to bed sleeping.

"Well, that was rude."

Jason popped out of his bed like a piece of bread shooting out of a toaster. When he saw Tillman in his room, he thought that it was an absolute invasion of his own privacy.

"Now you listen to me, Mr. Life Changer Extraordinaire. I am sick and tired of you coming to my house uninvited, and making rules that I don't want to do since I first lived here. You are nothing to me, do you hear me! I am commanding you to get this ankle bracelet off, get out of my apartment, and get out of my life!"

As Jason Edison tries to catch his breath with what he had to say to Tillman. The Life Changer had a few things to say to his client.

"I'm glad you got what you wanted to get off your chest, Mr. Edison, but now it's my turn to talk. My job is to change your life, and it is you who's making things difficult."

Jason wanted to give Tillman a piece of his mind. "What are you going to do, call my mommy? My parents don't give a crap about me!"

"You're wrong! They do care! Your girlfriend cared for you as well. What you're doing is shutting out everybody and everything connected to you."

"Why did you have to put an ankle bracelet on me and confine me to my apartment like I'm under house arrest? I have done nothing wrong to you."

"No, but you're the one who got in trouble with your neighbors and the police. I am here to give you a second chance in life."

"I rather stay in jail and face prison charges than watched over by a creep like you. Who would care about a loser like me besides a loser like you?"

Tillman gave the obvious answer. "The ones that you ignored the most are the ones who want to help you the most. I'm doing this to help your parents, your friends, and most of all, you."

"I never prayed for help, and I sure as heck didn't ask for it. I was too busy."

"Doing what, Jason?"

"Doing whatever I want. I was having a good time with my life before everybody got on my case."

All of a sudden, something seem to snap in Jason's mind. He wonders why Tillman came into his room while it was still locked.

"By the way, why are you in my room? How did you get inside with the door locked?"

Tillman answered. "On how I came in, I have my own ways. On why I'm in your room, dinner is being prepared."

"I'm not that hungry, but I am starving."

"Good, I had it ordered while you took a nap."

"You ordered a pizza?"

"No, Jason, I thought of something exquisite. I order us some steak."

"I don't know the last time I ever had steak."

"Wash up and get ready. Dinner is in ten minutes."

***

Moments later, Tillman set the table. He prepares the steak, baked potato, and salad for dinner. Jason came into the kitchen table looking forward to dinner.

Tillman acts like a maître d'. "Smoking or non-smoking, Mr. Edison?"

"I don't smoke when I eat. Nowadays, you can't smoke in a restaurant."

"Quite true, please have a seat."

Tillman blessed the Lord for the meal. Jason prayed along, he doesn't know the last time that he ever prayed, thinking that it was a waste of time. Tillman was getting the dressing for his salad, and saw Jason not touching his steak.

"Are you alright? You hardly touched your steak."

Jason wasn't sure. "There's nothing wrong with my steak. I mean, nobody ever fixed a steak for me in years."

"When was the last time you had a meal like this?"

"When I graduated high school. My parents took me to the nearest steakhouse, and we ordered the biggest steak they had."

"How big was the steak?"

"It was a good five pounder. Most steakhouses serve steaks that are bigger than that."

"Not to mention you have to finish the whole meal in a certain amount of time. They do that to win the prize money."

"I didn't do it for money. I went there to celebrate what I accomplished."

Jason took his knife and cut the steak to see how it was moist and juicy like it was in the steakhouse. However, as Jason took one bite of that steak, the memories started to haunt him. Tillman starts to worry about his client. He thought that Jason's story has something more to what Jason has said.

"Was there any memories about that night at the steakhouse?"

Jason continued eating, "I don't want to talk about it. I don't want to ruin a great meal."

The two continue eating their meals in silence. The atmosphere turned quiet for the next twenty minutes. Jason enjoyed his dinner and wondered if there was a dessert in the menu. Tillman didn't disappoint, he also brought in a key lime pie. Jason took a bite of it and thought it was amazing.

"You have to give me the recipe for this. This pie is delicious."

"You have to go to Florida for that. I know a great bakery a few miles short of Sarasota. They make a terrific key lime pie. I always order from them for special occasions."

After dinner, Jason decided to clean up. Tillman joined him, thinking what Jason said earlier today not helping him clean. Jason insisted he wanted to do this by himself. Tillman didn't interfere. After he clean and put the dishes in the drainer to dry. Jason went to the living room and cried with what was going on. Tillman thought the dinner must have brought some bad memories.

"There's something you haven't told me. Why did you have bad memories about it?"

Jason poured his heart out. "It wasn't the steakhouse, it was after the dinner."

Tillman sat next to Jason to find out what happened.

"After we had dinner, my parents were arguing later that night. I overheard everything my mom and dad fought about. My mom picked up the phone and she heard a voice that she doesn't know. She heard the woman who my dad was cheating with."

"Did your mom leave your dad after the argument?"

"She left him," Jason answered as he began to cry. "One time she called me on my birthday and I ask her when she will come back. She told me that she wasn't coming back."

Tillman looked in concern as Jason explained what happened. He listened as Jason poured his heart out with all the problems he had in the last four years.

"My dad was stricter since mom left. It's always his house and his rules. When I went to college, I was my own man. I was doing whatever I always wanted. Then I had problems with school, I partied more, and got kicked out. If you didn't come along, I would've been dead."

Tillman placed his arm around Jason's back as he wept. Tillman has seen something in Jason Edison that even Jason never had, compassion. Tillman wanted to ask his client a serious question.

"Do you want to change your life?"

Jason wiped the tears from his eyes. "I do. Please help me."

Tillman placed his hand on Jason's back and prayed for his client. Hoping that he would do anything to help Jason with what he's going through. After Tillman finished praying, Jason looked at him and asked.

"Lawrence, could you help me change my life?"

"We'll start first thing in the morning. Right now, we need to get to bed."

Jason headed off to bed. Knowing that tomorrow would be for him to be the start of something big. A chance for him to start all over.

***

The next day, Tillman act as an alarm for Jason. Jason wanted to kill his new alarm clock.

"Rise and shine, Jason. Ready for you to start over?"

Jason wanted to hit the snooze button. "C'mon, it's too early."

"Nonsense, it's a perfect day; I recommend you start eating your breakfast first."

Tillman placed a tray serving his client breakfast in bed. Jason is happy with what Tillman did for him.

"Wow, I'm surprised. The last time someone made me breakfast in bed was when I was seven."

"You had chickenpox at that time."

Jason looked at Tillman in shock. "Yes I did. You're not a psychic are you?"

Tillman laughed, "No. I thought it was a crazy hunch."

Tillman goes on telling Jason what was on the menu.

"I have prepared blueberry pancakes, scrambled eggs and sausage. Eat right now before you begin our plans."

"You don't have to tell me twice."

As Jason starts chowing down, he couldn't believe what Tillman did for him. Whatever Tillman has planned for him would be something out of the ordinary.

"What do you have planned in mind?"

"I was thinking that you need to get a job."

"A job?"

"Yes. I thought that with your case coming up, you could tell the judge you have been finding a job. The judge won't be as hard on you like your neighbors."

"It would be helpful if you remove my ankle bracelet."

"Consider it done."

Jason moved the tray aside, and pull down the covers to see the ankle bracelet was gone.

"How did you do that?"

"Like I said, I have my ways. Let's go."

As Jason got dressed, he and Tillman went outside the apartment. They were getting ready to head for the unemployment office. However, as Jason was getting ready to approach his car. He did not realize the oncoming car that hit him from out of nowhere. Tillman saw what happened and rushed to Jason's limp body by his side. Mr. Kowalski saw the whole thing happened and called 911 for an ambulance.

***

Jason is rush to the hospital on life support. He hasn't regained consciousness for a couple of days. The car that hit him felt like somebody punched him so hard the referee would count to one hundred. Tillman stayed with him, and prayed that he would be alright. Jason opened his eyes and saw Tillman there.

"Tillman, is that you?"

"It's me, Jason. You were out for a couple of days."

"What hit me?"

"A car."

Jason makes one simple request. "I want you to do something for me. I want you to ask God to forgive me for all my sins."

Tillman smiled. "I'll be glad to."

Tillman got on his knees praying to God to forgive Jason. When he prayed for Jason, he felt like he failed him.

Jason gives a faint whisper. "Don't grieve for me; you didn't fail me. I'm the one who failed you."

"No, Jason. You didn't fail me."

"I hope that God will forgive me."

"He will. All you have to do is believe in Him, and He'll forgive you."

Jason makes a proclamation. "I do believe. I don't want to spend my life in hell for all eternity."

As Jason held Tillman's hand, he flatlined to his death. Doctors try to revive Jason, but to no avail. Jason Edison was dead. Lawrence Tillman left Jason's hospital room. He turned around and saw two police officers talk to the doctors outside the door. It turns out they found the license plate on the hit and run. The police found out the driver of the car was dead on arrival. The ambulance technicians brought the stretcher out with a tag on the toe. The tag reads:

Edison, Jason

As the flatline from Jason's room grew louder and louder, he wakes up. The noise came from his alarm clock. Jason was alive and well in his apartment. He saw the ashtray that has the put-out joint. He took the ashtray along with his secret stash and dumped it all in the toilet. He then knocked on Kowalski's door. Kowalski looked like in he was in a bad mood, but he saw Jason in tears asking if he could use his phone.

Kowalski looked at Jason like he was feeling sick, and decided to let him use the phone. Jason called the only person who would only help him.

"Hello, dad."

Jason cried out to him asking if he wanted to help him. Jason's father knew the tears from his son, feeling the same way his mom felt since the divorce. His dad tells Jason that he would do everything to help his son, and was happy that he called him. In the end, Jason got on his knees and not only prayed to God for forgiveness. He also wanted to thank Tillman for helping him get his life back on track. Even Kowalski helped him pray.

Jason Edison knew that second chances are hard to come by. When somebody offers a person a chance to turn his life around; it would take a sinner to pray for repentance and know that he will be forgiven. We need to forgive others as Jesus forgave us when he died on the cross paying for the sins of the world. Forgiveness is only a sin, and a prayer away.

Sin #5 WRATH

Out of all the seven deadly sins, this is the most powerful, and the most dangerous. Let's face it, we get angry sometimes, but if the anger gets big, it can lead to serious problems. Whether its name calling, insults, Anti-Semitism, racism, stereotyping, prejudice, or even worse; war!

You heard about people of hate throughout history; Hitler, Saddam, Osama. They got away with killing people, invading countries, and making threats saying they're better than us. There is a place for people who cause fear to their people, fear to all humanity, and even fear to one's self. It's called Hell, and those three dictators are already there. In my next tale, somebody might be going there with them.

My next story deals with a corrupt politician who is running for President. And spreads a trail of hate and fear in a southern town, with some unassisted help of course. I call this story:

THE DEVIL'S CANDIDATE

The Devil's Candidate
A Tale of Wrath

I t was a hot summer's day in Mobile, Alabama. The temperature was a scorching ninety-eight degrees. The townspeople try to cool themselves with a cold drink on the front porch. Youngsters try to cool off at a swimming hole, and other people thought the weather was perfect for an all-over tan. However, the hottest spot in the Heart of Dixie is outside the steps of the county courthouse. Former Governor Jacob Borden is making a campaign stop on his run for President of the United States.

"My fellow Americans, for the last eight years, we've made countless attempts of getting this country back on its feet. The people in Washington have bailed out big businesses with your hard-earned money."

The crowd was paying attention to Borden's speech. Some of the people admired him because he looked like a younger version of John F. Kennedy.

"Are you happy with the way things are?"

The crowd shouted with a big no. Knowing the last few years were dismal to this country. As the Governor continues to talk, an angry mob marches down to the courthouse in a rally of protest.

The Governor looked at the angry crowd. "Can I help you?"

Enter Allan Henegan, a southern baptist preacher who can preach the gospel in a single breath. He stands at the same step the Governor was standing looking him right in the eyes.

"There's one thing you can do for us, Governor. You can take your campaign, and leave these fine people in Mobile alone!"

Henegan's crowd held signs that say, "Go Home Racist!", and "Borden should get the ax!" State troopers escorted out Borden and his staff. The crowd kept booing at the Governor until he and his staff got into the limousine. Governor Borden's campaign manager, Terry Winslow was not in the best of mood.

"Well, this is great! If the media finds out about this little fiasco, we can kiss the presidency good-bye!"

The Governor became desperate. "Tell me something I don't know. That's the third town this week. I've never face that much disrespect since I first became Governor."

Terry hates being the one in charge of damage control. "We'll fix this little problem, Governor."

The limo heads back to the hotel for a special emergency meeting. Unbeknownst to the Governor, another limousine was following him. This limo was candy apple red; the passenger looked at his TV, and tells his driver to wait until dark.

***

Hours later, the Governor watched the news along with his campaign staff. Allyson Sanford, the local news reporter interviewed Allan Hennegan about the protest.

"Why did you protest Governor Borden's speech?"

Allan gave the young reporter his answer. "Because I have conclusive proof that Jacob Borden was once a member of the Ku Klux Klan."

The cat was out of the bag, the Governor has hidden his secret of hate for so long. His campaign team is in shock by this announcement. Borden felt like he got knocked out by a sucker punch. He now knows there's nothing he or his team can do about it.

Terry looked at his boss. "Governor, is it true what Henegan said?"

Governor Borden looked like he was getting ready to explode. He looked at his staff and shocked them all by saying the one thing he kept all these years ago.

"Yes, I was with the Klan! Alright! You all want the truth; you got it! I was a member of the Klan! Now my whole campaign is on a trail of destruction because of that preacher!"

After he shouted his confession, the Governor heads to his room as he broke down in tears and cried. Terry followed him.

"I lost everything, Terry. Nothing can pull me back."

"Oh, I wouldn't say that."

"Who's there?"

The Governor turns to see a tall thin man dressed in a red suit standing at the door. Borden was not in the mood to see anyone, especially when someone appears out of nowhere.

"Who are you?"

The stranger introduced himself. "The name is DeVille, Damien DeVille. I'm here to help you."

Borden didn't want any help. "Well you're too late for that."

"Nonsense. I heard about your little problem outside the courthouse. So I asked the receptionist where you're staying, and here I am."

Terry tells Damien to go away. "That's nice of you, but we don't need a new image maker."

Damien looks at Terry and tells him what he thinks of his remark.

"I am not an image maker, Mr. Winslow. I'm more of a career maker. If you don't mind, I like to talk to the Governor alone."

Before Terry tries to get another word in edgewise, Damien looks at him with his glowing red eyes. Terry decided to leave the Governor's room. Once Terry was gone, the Governor and DeVille can finally get down to business.

The Governor is in denial. "Who do you think you are, my tax advisor?"

Damien laughed. "No, I'm here to help you win the presidency."

Governor Borden laughed at Damien. He thought there's no way somebody like Damien can help him be president. Damien is very serious.

"I can help you win. All you have to do is you do as I say, and the power and prestige will be yours."

"What's the catch?"

"No catch," Damien opened his briefcase. "Sign this, and your little problem can go away."

"What if I say no?"

"Then you'll face the same problems as today. You'll be the target of the media, the minorities, even your own political cohorts."

"You can't take a problem like mine and make it disappear like a magic trick."

"You're right, I am not a magician. I'm more of an agent."

Governor Borden hung his head down low thinking he could use a drink. Damien gazed at a bottle of scotch on the table. As he poured the scotch, he added a little something extra to make the Governor more relaxed. The Governor drank his scotch slow as the potion calmed him down. An evil smile spreads across Damien's face.

"Are you feeling calm, Governor?"

The Governor starts to mellow out. "That depends. Do you have any more of this scotch?"

Damien had other ideas. "Now, Jacob. I need you to be more relaxed, not drunk."

Damien gives the Governor the contract and tells him to sign on the dotted line. After the Governor signed the contract, he went to sleep. Damien tucked him in like a mother to her child and told him not to worry; the problem will go away tomorrow. As for Damien DeVille, the fun is about to begin.

***

The next morning, the telephone was ringing off the hook. Governor Jacob Borden got up feeling miserable due to a hangover. He picked up the phone.

"Hello."

Terry was on the other line, he was livid.

"It's about time you woke up. Do you have any idea what the heck is going on with the campaign!"

If the hangover was not enough for the Governor, Terry's shouting made it worse.

"Will you stop yelling at me! I have a massive hangover and I can't take any more pain."

"Well excuse me, Prince Charming. Are you watching TV right now?"

"I'm trying to get up, Terry. I haven't had the time to turn on the TV."

"Well turn it on, Mr. Future President. It's on every news channel."

"Is this your idea of a joke? I don't find it funny."

Terry was serious. "Turn on the TV."

The Governor turns on the TV, and news came in that Jacob Borden won the primary for the state of Alabama. The report about him being a Klansmen was like a faded memory.

A familiar voice told Borden not to worry. "I told you I can help you win, son."

Governor Borden turned around and saw Damien DeVille with a bottle of champagne. Damien looks at the stunned Governor with a sinister smile.

"All you have to do is trust me."

Governor Borden is not impressed. "I don't know what you did, but you're not getting away with this."

Damien felt hurt. "Aw, Governor, I'm crushed. I try to help you and you're throwing me to the curb."

"Problems don't go away by waving a magic wand. What you did made things worse."

"You would've lost the primary as well as the election if it weren't for me. Admit it, Jacob, without me you're nothing."

Governor Borden continued looking at the news. He heard that Allan Henegan died last night from a series of stab wounds. Borden is in shock to find out that his protestor was dead, but he knows who's behind the incident.

"It was you, wasn't it?" he stared at Damien. "I would have you arrested for murder."

Damien had other things in mind. "You call the police, and I'll tell them you hired me to kill Henegan. In the meantime, you'll do as I say and your life might have some meaning. Besides, you signed a contract for my services."

The Governor began to laugh. "What do you mean I signed a contract with you? I would have to be drunk to do something stupid."

Damien laughed at Jacob's remark. The Governor figured out what happened to him last night.

"You put something in my drink."

"Ding! Ding! Ding! We have a winner! I told you without me, you're nothing."

Borden clenched his fist with rage. "I want to see the contract, and I want to see it now!"

Without warning, the telephone rang. Governor Borden picked up the phone. He turns around and notices that Damien has vanished.

The Governor said, "Hello."

Terry was on the phone asking where the Governor was, the press wanted to ask him a few questions. Borden tells his campaign manager that he'll be right there. Borden puts on his jacket and heads to the conference. He made sure he kept his mind on the campaign, and not on Damien DeVille.

Governor Borden headed to a lion's den. A pack of reporters asked him about his connection with the Klan as well as the death of Allan Henegan. The Governor pulled no punches with the questions. He explained he couldn't change what he did in the past. He also stated he had nothing to do with Reverend Henegan's death. He hoped the next stop of the campaign would be a lot better than what happened.

After the conference, some of Borden's staff is in astonishment with the way he handled the press. All a sudden, Governor Borden saw Damien with a couple of hot young models. He decided he needs a word with his new benefactor.

"Might I have a brief word with you?"

Damien was busy. "Not now, I'm busy with these Southern Belles here."

The Governor thought of something quick to get Damien's attention.

"In that case, the deal is off."

As the Governor walked away, Damien saw him packing his bags for the next campaign. He was angry with the Governor.

"What do you mean the deal is off!"

Borden was cool as a cucumber. "I wanted to get your attention. After what happened, I don't need you anymore."

"That's when you're wrong, Governor! Once you signed the contract, it states that I'm going to help you whether you like it or not. If you ever call off this deal, I swear I will make your life miserable. Don't you ever forget it!"

"Who do you think you are, Buster?"

"I'm the last person you'd want to mess with. I'll see you around."

As Damien walked out, Governor Borden gets ready to head for the next stop in his campaign. After he saw his mysterious benefactor walked out of the hotel with the two hot ladies. Governor Borden looked at the contract to find a loophole. Terry tells the Governor that it's time to go. The Governor knew that where he's going, Hell is not far behind.

***

Days later, Governor Jacob Borden continued his campaign tour. And on every stop, he continues to deal with anti-hate groups and controversy. Damien DeVille shows up making sure Borden will get the vote by any means necessary. At the National Convention, Jacob Borden was the party's nominee. Governor Borden couldn't believe what has happen to him. DeVille laughed with delight, because his new client is now the party's candidate.

***

A few days later, Governor Borden got a phone call from Damien asking to see him in private. Terry went to his boss to talk to him before he leaves.

"Governor, I need to talk to you. It's about your so-called mysterious benefactor."

"If you have a problem with campaign supporters, you should talk to them."

"I tried to get in touch with Damien, but all I got from him is nothing. No phone numbers, no word on where he stays, and I called every limousine rental place in the country."

Borden becomes confused. "Why in the world did you call every limousine rental place in the country?"

"I did that for two obvious reasons. The first is to find out if they rent any candy apple red limousines for Damien. The second is to get Damien's phone number. I even imitated Damien much to no avail."

"What do you find out?"

"They don't have any red limousines to rent. He must have brought the limo with him."

Governor Borden is now concerned. He not only has a problem with whom Damien DeVille is, but why does he want him to win the presidency. He needs to get ready for his first debate with his new opponent, and he needs all the rest he could get.

***

A few months have passed, and on a cold January 20th in Washington D.C.. Governor Jacob Borden is sworn in as President of the United States. Borden begins to speak in front of a crowd of millions.

"My fellow Americans, we are standing here on a day of greatness. We stand today in a new era, and we will do everything to make this country the strongest nation on Earth."

Applause came in like the sound of roaring thunder as Borden continues his speech.

"We will do everything in our power to make sure we will not go in defeat."

All of a sudden, Borden spotted a group of protestors. They held signs saying, "Impeach Borden, NOW!" and "America can't afford to be under Klan law."

Borden looked at the protestors. "Can I help you?"

One protestor was the spokesman for the group. "Oh there's one thing you can do for everybody, Mr. President."

The protestor steps forward and President Borden is in shock to see who it was. It was Allan Henegan, and he had a message to give to the president.

"We don't want you running this country, Mr. President. In fact, we're taking you out."

Borden saw thousands of men who he hated all his life, like a scene from a bad horror movie. He ran to the inside of the Capitol Building.

Members of both the house & senate chased Borden as well as the protestors. Borden heads to the rotunda, surrounded by a group of protestors. As the protestors close in on the President, a huge alarm blared out, but it was more than a terrorist threat. It was a nightmare.

***

The alarm was nothing but the clock on Borden's hotel room, the Governor woke up in a pool of sweat. The election is two months away, and the stakes have never been higher. Governor Borden went downstairs to get a cup of strong black coffee & a bran muffin. He saw Damien DeVille stopping by, and his benefactor was not in a real good mood.

"Why didn't you see me last night, Governor?"

"Leave me alone, I don't want to see you, anymore."

Damien couldn't take no for an answer. He followed the Governor up to his hotel room and comes in to confront Borden.

"Let me tell you one thing, Governor. Nobody walks out on Damien DeVille, nobody!"

"Well let me be the first to say, goodbye! I'm thru with the way this campaign is going, I want you out of here, and the contract between you and me is over!"

Damien thought otherwise. "Oh, I don't think so. When you signed the contract, it states you belong to me between now and the hereafter."

Borden thought Damien was joking. "Are you telling me that I've sold my soul to become President of the United States?"

Damien laughs at Governor Borden's question. "You figured it out, magnificent. You've got to be a sucker."

"I don't have to be a genius to figure out who you are."

"And what exactly is that, Governor?"

Governor Borden looked as he walks towards Damien and tells him who he is.

"I know that you are nothing but the devil himself."

Damien smiles at the Governor and applauded. "Bravo, you've finally figured me out. You must be a psychic."

"You're nothing but an absolute sicko. I don't want to be with you. I don't want anything to do with you. I don't want you near me or my campaign. I want you out of my life!"

"Very well, Governor."

As he heads towards the door, Damien turned to look at an angry Jacob Borden and gives him a simple reminder.

"Remember this, Governor. You signed the contract, which means you are mine, forever."

Damien DeVille left Governor Borden's hotel room laughing like a maniac as Terry comes in concerned.

"What happened between you and Damien? Why did he come out of your room laughing?"

Governor Borden looked at his campaign manager, and tells him to sit down.

"Terry, that guy who came out of my room is not what you or anybody else thinks of Damien."

"Who is he, a comedian?"

"No, worse. I made a deal with the devil."

Terry laughed like crazy with what the Governor said. Borden wasn't happy with Terry's laugh.

"This is not funny, Terry! I signed a contract with Damien!"

"I'm sorry, Governor, but I thought what you said made me laugh."

"I'm telling you the truth. Damien DeVille is the devil, and I have the contract where I signed with him. He drugged me to sign it."

Terry looked at his boss in concern. "Could I look at the contract?"

Jacob takes out the contract he signed from Damien and gives it to Terry. The Governor wondered why Terry wanted to look at the contract.

"I don't mean to be a worry wart, but why are you examining the contract?"

"I'm looking for every flaw, catch, or loophole in this stupid contract, because there is no way for Damien to win."

"What do you want me to tell for the debate?"

Terry gives the Governor a piece of advice. "As your campaign manager, I would tell you to be yourself. As a Christian, I would tell you that you should pray to God for forgiveness."

"I do pray to God for forgiveness, but I don't think he'll ever take a person like me."

"What you did back then is all in the past. It's time for you to face your own future. And the way you'll do it is to put your problems in God's hands, not Damien's."

Governor Borden got down on his knees, and prayed for forgiveness. Terry kneeled by his employer's side making sure he surrenders his life to the Lord. Borden tells in his prayer how many bad choices he made in his life. As he continued to confess his sins, he asked God to forgive him for every bad decision. After the prayer, there was a knock at the door. It was the bellhop telling the Governor the limo was waiting at the parking lot to take him to the debate. Borden told the bellhop he'll be right down.

The Governor told his manager thanks. "You know, Terry. I'm feeling a lot better, thank you."

"I only have one more suggestion for you, Governor. Tell the truth, and get back to where you're accepted as a candidate and as a human being."

Borden smiled and said, "That's exactly what I'll do. Thank you, Terry, for everything. I'm going to win this debate."

Governor Jacob Borden walked down to the limousine with a new lease on life as he goes to the town hall for the debate. What he plans to deal with his life is up to him. The phone in the limousine started to ring, and Borden picks it up.

"Hello."

Damien DeVille was on the other line. And from what the Governor heard, he was furious.

"Hello, Governor. I'm outside the town hall today for the debate. I'm wondering if you want to hit the town afterwards."

The Governor had other plans. "Forget it, DeVille, effective immediately; I'm no longer in business with you."

"Don't you ever say that to me, Borden! Do you know who you are talking to!"

"Yes I do. I'm talking to a washed-up, no talent loser who shouldn't interfere with my campaign. And if I ever see you try to get somebody to sell their souls for your own merriment, I will tell them who you are. GOOD-BYE!"

As he hung up the phone, the Governor thought his argument with Damien felt pretty good. The driver asked Borden who he was yelling at over the phone. Borden tells the driver the caller was a nobody.

"Are you okay, Governor?"

"Oh, I'm fine. I made a clean slate for the Lord, today and forever."

As the limo arrived at the town hall for the Presidential Debate, Governor Borden gave the driver $200 as a tip. The driver is in shock to see Borden in a better mood. Governor Borden enters the town hall to a mixed reaction from the crowd. He headed to the dressing room where he saw his opponent, a young US Senator named Ronald Murphy. The two were getting ready as the candidates shake hands and prepare for the debate.

The moderator comes in and asked the questions involving the problems with this country. The two candidates explain each topic with such passion. After the topics, they each have a closing argument. Senator Murphy went first.

"Ladies & Gentlemen, we are facing hard times in our nation today. However, there will come a time when we face a change in our lives and our future, the time for change is now."

Then it was time for Governor Borden to speak, he got nervous as he spoke to the crowd.

"Ladies & Gentlemen, over the past few months I'm called a lot of things, and as a racist because of my past. I'm here to tell you, I agree with what my opponent said. In order for us to face the changes in this country, we need to change as well. We need to change the way we act towards ourselves and each other. And changing the world starts with one person, that one person is you."

The crowd applauded with what Governor Borden said. Even the crowd who protested are in a state of surprise with Borden's closing argument. They seem to notice that Borden became a changed man. The two candidates shook hands as the debate was over.

"I asked God to forgive me for all my sins," said the Governor. "I hope this is a real start for me."

The Senator replied, "You're already forgiven, by the people and by me."

"And whether I win the presidency or not," Borden said, "I'm already a winner, in the eyes of the Lord."

"Amen to that, Jacob," said Ronald, "amen to that."

The two left the stage together as they head to their campaign staff. Even Senator Murphy's campaign manager is happy with the way Borden explained his actions.

As the Governor walked out of town hall, a crowd of people applauded him for what he said. And as he signed a few autographs, a young black man stood in front of the Governor with a gun in his hand.

"Die, you Nazi cracker!"

Borden's campaign supporters screamed as the Governor took six bullets to the chest and lie down on the floor. The police captured the assassin soon afterwards. Senator Murphy held the Governor's hand as the ambulance arrives. The Governor asked his opponent an important question.

"Do you think... I'll go... to Heaven?"

Senator Murphy continued holding his opponent. "As of now, you are on your way there."

Senator Ronald Murphy watched his political adversary die in the middle of the street. The country stood in complete silence. Meanwhile, on the outskirts of town, Damien watched the news on his cell phone that his client was dead. But he was angry to find out that he was going to Heaven, the contract was null & void.

All of a sudden, he gets a phone call from his boss about another lost soul like Borden's in another city. He got in his candy apple red limousine and is on his way, laughing. Wherever there is hate or prejudice, he's always there causing his own way of trouble. Keep your eyes open for a candy apple red long stretch limousine with a license plate that reads 666. He's here because we keep him through hate & fear. Don't you be another lost soul.

PRESTON DAMERON

Sin #6 ENVY

Color our next deadly sin, green. This sin deals with jealousy, and what I'm about to tell you might even shock you.

We're all jealous in one form or another. Do you look outside and you see your next door neighbor riding around town in a new car? Or do you see your neighbor enjoying a movie on a 50" High Definition TV set with a fancy Blu-Ray home theater system and you view the same film on a standard TV? And while you went to the world's biggest Polish Sausage Festival on your vacation, your neighbor spent his summer vacation traveling Around the World. These are more than mere dramatizations, but before you get jealous, I'll give you this friendly advice. Don't keep up with the Joneses, because they're always broke!

That is what envy is, it's nothing but a game of "Can You Top This." And every time you try to play this game, it would hurt you and your finances in the long run. Case in point, the people in my next tale. It's about two brothers who kept playing a 1-up game against each other, but the results are nasty. I call this modern day Cain & Abel story:

SEARCHING FOR THE CURE

Searching for the Cure
A Tale of Envy

"**M**y brother is a creep." Those were the words of Jeff Hagen, who is talking to detectives about the death of his brother, Tim. Leon Grendel, the lead detective of the case questioned why Jeff said those words.

"Is that why you murder him, Mr. Hagen?"

"That's not true. I may hate my brother, but I didn't kill him."

Grendel's partner, Detective James Malloy found strong evidence against the former football star. "Listen, Hagen, forensics checked the bullets that killed your brother. They came from the same gun found in your lock box."

"I said I didn't kill my brother!"

Grendel added more evidence. "We also checked the gun for fingerprints, along with your own. They're an exact match. So you better have a real explanation why your brother is dead."

"I kept the lock box under my bed, did you checked the fingerprints on that you Joe Friday wannabes?"

Grendel gets mad. "You shut your mouth, Hagen. We checked the gun box as well as the lock. The fingerprints we found are the same as your gun."

"I had the key with me at all times. I swear to God I didn't have the key with me."

Malloy had an idea. "Why don't you tell your story from the beginning. Perchance there's a way to clear your name."

Jeff Hagen is in a bad predicament, he's accused of the murder of his brother, and the odds are bad for him. The only way for Jeff to get out of this pickle is to tell his side of the story.

"The truth is we despise one another since we were children. When I was three, I was angry when my parents told me I was going to have a brother or sister."

Grendel listened. "So you wanted be the only child in your family. You always wanted to get more attention. The classic case of sibling rivalry, and you were the Cain to Tim's Abel."

"Sometimes I wanted to kill him when mom & dad aren't around; I wasn't happy on how they treated Tim from the beginning."

Malloy figured what was obvious. "So your folks treated Tim better than they treated you. A classic case of sibling rivalry every psychologist can understand."

"It's not about sibling rivalry! You both sound like I'm competing with him."

Grendel slammed his hand on the table. "Reality check, Mr. All-American. You have been in competition since you were children."

"That was then!"

Jeff's confession to the detectives was more than a plea. Once Tim was born, the two brothers have been playing one-up against each other. Both exceeded in school, Jeff competed in football and track receiving awards for his work. Tim became an expert in chess and written scientific theories at the age of fifteen. Theories most scientists believe were preposterous. Tim skipped to the senior class, which made Jeff angry. When they graduated from high school, the Hagen brothers went their separate ways. Jeff became the frat boy type while Tim followed the path to success, a path that became a long hard road. Both brothers graduated with Jeff as an underpaid pro football player. Tim became the youngest research scientist in the school's science department.

Both Grendel & Malloy try to figure out why the rivalry turned deadly since Tim died. Why was Jeff at the scene of the crime? And what was the cause of Tim's death? Detective Grendel asked Jeff a harsh question.

"What I like to know is what happened on the night that your brother died?"

Jeff maintained his innocence. "I told you, I have no idea why Tim was dead. I saw the body before you guys caught me."

"Do you hate your brother, Mr. Hagen?"

With a tear rolling down his face, Jeff gave his answer in a whisper. "No."

The detectives couldn't hear what Jeff said, and asked him to speak a little louder.

"I said NO, you stupid badge kissers!"

Grendel wants to go over the table and destroy the former football player with his bare hands. Malloy prevented his partner from doing that.

"Lemme at him, Malloy, I'm gonna teach this has-been some manners!"

"And risk losing your badge. I have a better way, Leon. Let me handle this."

"What do you want me to do, sing Kumbaya?"

"No, get us some coffee. It's going to be a long night."

Malloy looked at Jeff sitting there by himself. Knowing he hasn't had anything to eat or drink after the arrest.

"How do you like your coffee, Mr. Hagen?"

Jeff acted like a jerk. "I'll take it with a shot of whiskey."

Grendel didn't buy it. "Cut the crap, has-been! How do you really take your coffee?"

"Black, alright! I take my coffee black!"

Grendel left the room in anger leaving his rookie partner handles his hot-headed suspect. Jeff couldn't believe Malloy sitting there acting calm.

"You're always quiet; I couldn't believe you prevented your partner from killing me."

"Don't take it personal, Mr. Hagen. I was in the top of my class when it comes to interrogating criminals."

"I am not a criminal; I don't know why I'm in jail for something I didn't do."

"I'm a firm believer in someone who's innocent until proven guilty. So we have a lot in common."

Jeff couldn't believe what the young detective said. "What are you, a comedian?"

"No, Mr. Hagen, I'm a Christian."

"You don't look like a Christian to me. You chose being a cop over your faith."

"That's when you're wrong. My job and my family are important, Mr. Hagen. Without God showing me how to handle justice; I wouldn't be talking to you. I go to church before I go on duty."

"I'm in need of serious praying," said Jeff. "I haven't got much sleep since my arrest."

Malloy had a thought, if he thinks that Jeff is being truthful, he must know what lead to Tim's murder.

"Okay, Mr. Hagen, how about we start from the beginning."

Jeff didn't want to go over it. "Look, detective. If I keep talking about our childhood, I would put you to sleep."

"No, I don't mean from your beginning. I want to know what happened the days before your brother's murder."

"If I told you once, I told you a zillion times. I didn't kill my brother."

"I know you told us. I want to know what happened."

Jeff is now between a rock and a hard place. He knows in his heart that he didn't kill his little brother. However, he needed to prove his innocence to Detective Malloy. Jeff explained the actions that happened before the murder.

***

It all started three days ago. After my football career ended, I became the high school's new assistant football coach. I was teaching young talent to become leaders and role models for our community. I was finishing football practice when I got a phone call from my father. He told me that Tim was coming over to visit, and he's bringing somebody with him.

I haven't seen my brother since my wedding. At first, I thought he was too busy to show up. Nevertheless, I never expected to see Tim at my wedding. While my marriage and my football career went down the tubes. My brother received accolades and awards for his scientific theories. I thought he was the biggest dork in the universe. So, when I'm asked if I'm related to somebody as smart as my brother, I would tell them no.

When practice was over, I went to the convenience store and bought a case of beer, and I headed off to my parent's house. I saw my brother's car on the driveway blocking me to get in. When I parked on the street, I brought the beer with me. I was about to give my little brother a piece of my mind.

"What's the big idea having your clown car blocking the driveway!"

My brother looked at me and gave me a stupid remark.

"It's nice to see you again, Jeff."

Tim wasn't alone this time. I thought he brought another stupid science trophy. Instead, he has somebody with him. When I saw my brother's new assistant, she was not who I thought she'd be. She may have the brains of a scientist, but she's got the body of a tramp.

"You must be Jeff, your brother told me about you."

I tried to woo her. "Well then, what did my kind little brother say about me?"

Her answer is a rude awakening. "Like a kiddie pool. Shallow."

Who is this ungrateful bimbo calling me shallow? I was an All-American for crying out loud! Luckily, my brother has the common courtesy to introduce her.

"My dear brother, where are my manners," said Tim, "I like to introduce you to Dr. Lisa Van Janssen. She's my research assistant on a project that would revolutionize the medical field."

"Let me guess. Why dorky scientists like you couldn't get any."

Lisa fired back. "No, that would be what you're dealing with since your divorce. We are going to create the cure for the plague of the 21st century."

My mother, Lillian wanted to know. "What plague are you talking about, sweetie?"

My brother gave her the answer. "Mom, we are going to cure cancer."

My mom & dad were happy about the good news. However, I wasn't thrilled with it. I never thought my brother is going to turn the scientific community upside down. I mean I'd be happy for my brother making that huge announcement. We both lost friends and family to cancer. I don't know what he would do next to almost every incurable disease. I was jealous of my brother, and I'm even more jealous of his new assistant. Why someone who can be this sexy would be so dorky, especially when she hangs around with Super Spaz? My parents insisted we go out to dinner together. I thought of something quick to get away from my geeky little brother and his even geekier assistant.

"I can't tonight; I have to get ready for game night tomorrow."

My father threw a wrench at my excuse.

"Nonsense, this calls for a celebration. I want for all of us to go out for dinner."

My brother played the family card. "I agree, father. Besides, when was the last time the four of us ever got the chance to celebrate?"

Lisa wanted to join in. "I hope I get to take part of the celebration. It'll give me the opportunity to get to know everybody."

I couldn't take more of this. "That's great. I thought things would've been better when I was the only child."

I headed to my car. My mother was heartbroken with the way I acted. I didn't want to be with my brother for one minute longer.

Lisa felt sorry for my brother. "Is your brother always like that to you, Tim?"

Tim gave his new assistant his answer. "Not all the time, only if it involves drinking."

Lisa turned to my mother. "Mrs. Hagen, I don't feel like going to dinner, either. I'll be going to the hotel."

My mom wouldn't take no for an answer. "Nonsense, Lisa, If you are going to be part of our happy family, you need to get to know us like you have with Tim."

"What if Jeff comes back? Will he be more of a problem?"

"No, dearie, he hasn't been the same since his pro career ended."

"I didn't know he played pro football."

Tim concurred for his assistant. "Oh, he did, his career lasted the whole pre-season."

My dad butts in. "That's not true, Tim. He did play more than the pre-season."

"Dad, he spent most of the season on the bench. After that, his season was over."

Mom added her two cents. "Not to mention the other teams didn't want him after his arrest."

Dad didn't want to hear about the arrest, and I would agree if I was around. I don't like it when people talk behind my back. They went out to have dinner while I drove back to my house. I worked on some plays out for Friday's game. I looked at the team's game footage from last week's game as I drink my beer. I kept thinking about what my brother would succeed in finding the cure for cancer. I mean he would be the toast of the scientific community. Every journal of medicine would mention his success. Not to mention receiving the Nobel Prize if his theory is correct. That would get me so angry that I wanted to do something horrible to him. I was the big deal in the Hagen family, me! I get to play once every Sunday so everyone can see me. What did I get in return? Being benched for no reason, and losing my job once the season's over. They always treat my brother as if he was more special than me.

Out of the blue, I got a phone call from my brother. He asked me if I changed my mind about coming down to the Porker Pit for dinner. I said that I wanted to be alone, so I hanged up the phone. It was clear that I don't want to talk to him, be with him, let alone live with him. Two minutes later, the phone rang, and I was about to give my pesky little brother another piece of my mind.

"Listen here, I'm tired of you calling me to bother me."

However, the voice on the other end of my phone call was a different kind of pest.

"Are you talking to me, or your brother?"

It was Lisa, dork 2 to my brother's dork 1.

"What do you want?"

"I want to know why you acted like a jerk to your brother like what you're doing to me."

If there's one thing I hate worse than one dorkasaurus, it's another dorkasaurus who could be hot in bed. Especially if she's with a stud muffin like me.

"You want to know why I act this way."

"I do have the right to know."

"Because I can!"

I laughed at Lisa's reply as she hung up the phone in disgust.

I'll admit, I love making my brother's friends more miserable than him. She told my brother what I said to her. My brother called me from his car and gave me a mouthful of hot air. Jeez, can't my dorky little brother ever take a joke? From his point of view, no way. That's my brother for you, I'd never try to fill his shoes at all. And if he tries to fill my shoes on the gridiron, I guarantee he'd become compost.

I saw a car came by my driveway, it was my brother. How the heck did he find my address? Did he place one of those tracking devices in my car to find me? He knocked on the door so loud that he wanted to bust out down. I opened the door and wanted to do to him like my ex-wives' lawyers.

"Go away, you pest!" I shouted as I slammed the door.

My brother continued knocking on the door. I mean anyone who has a little brother who keeps bugging their older sibling would have to feel for me. I open the door, but he was gone. I smiled seeing the little creep out of my hair, and out of my life. And as I closed the door, I heard a voice even worse than my ex-wife.

"Are you always a creep?"

It was Tim, and he looks like a victim of a wedgie dealt by me.

"How did you get in my house?" I asked. "And how did you know where I live?"

"Well, that's easy," said my pesky little brother. "Mom told me where you live, and as far as getting in; she gave me the key."

Tim looked at me like he was dealing with a bully, and the bully was me.

"My assistant is angry with the way you treated her over the phone."

"That is not my problem."

"If it deals with people who I work or have business with, it concerns me. What you're doing is your problem. No wonder your career and your marriages went down faster than the Titanic."

"Are you done boring me to death?"

"No, big brother, I'm getting started. You don't know what bored to death is."

He was right, I thought I hit rock bottom was when the Vipers released me. Hoping I would get a chance to play football with another team. When I was little, I always wanted to play for my favorite team, the

Detroit Mephistos. But during the off season, the record I didn't want would not give me a chance to sign me up. In fact, the rest of the league couldn't accept me for the times I spent in jail. The news traveled around the league like an ugly rumor in a supermarket tabloid. My career was over before I ever got the chance to get it started.

Tim had one reason why he's here. "I didn't come here to start a fight with you, Jeff. I come here to ask you for advice."

I looked at my brother in confusion. "Now how in the world can you ask somebody who treated you like slime for advice?"

"I want to ask you about getting married."

"What!"

"I was afraid to pop the question to Lisa. I need some advice and I couldn't ask mom or dad about it, so I needed an outside source."

Oh, my gosh! I can't believe what I've heard from my little brother. He wants to get married to his assistant, and even though I'm proud of him for what he's doing. There's no doubt that he's rushing things like I was when I got married. I needed to be honest to Tim.

"It's not the right time to pop the question to Lisa."

"But Jeff, I need someone I can trust with what I'm going to do."

"Tim, I'm telling you from experience, I went to the alter twice, and they both didn't turn out good. I do think Lisa's a great girl even though she's your equal, but I also believe now is not the right time."

Even though I treated my brother like a cockroach that wouldn't stay dead. I tried to save him from making a serious mistake by marrying Lisa. And if he found the cure for cancer like he said he has, he would have to deal with success first.

Jeff came to his senses. "You're right, what was I thinking. I need to get back and continue my research."

"Don't apologize, bro. I do think you need to think about this."

Tim gave me a hug and wished me thanks. As he left, I went back to drink my beer, and continue taking notes on the game film. Deep down, even though Tim is nothing but a pest, he's still my brother. I thought what he's doing is a serious step. As his brother, I prevented him from making a huge mistake. Heck, I wish he was around to help me when I went through rough times of my own. I was jealous of him for all these years. I decided to turn off the video, and go straight to bed.

***

The next day, it was business as usual. I instructed some of the players on new plays for our homecoming game. Every year since I played, we always got our butts kicked. The last year was a disaster; we not only lost to our opponents. We also loss to the mud and heavy rain which cause us to fumble more times than a team of pee-wee players. I didn't expect a certain visitor to drop by the school. My brother shows up and saw me coaching, which made me ill. However, he did keep his distance as he watched from afar. I'm surprised we didn't use him as a tackling dummy when I played. Mom would've kill me for that. Tim waved hello to me before heading to the school. Some waterboy looked at him in a suspicious manner; he asked me if that was my brother. I gave him this reply.

"You're not filling those bottles enough. Get to it."

Tim would take pity on the kid even though he was a dork. He would not be happy with how I dealt with the waterboy. I decided to tell him the truth.

"Hey, kid. Look, I want to apologize to you. That is my brother."

"I wanted to ask him about becoming a scientist."

"What type of science are you interested in?"

"I'm interested in sports science."

"Sounds interesting, I'll talk to him what he thinks about it. If I can't, talk to your science teachers about it."

The waterboy got excited. "I will. Thanks, coach."

I mentor my teammates into leaders in their own mind, and the odds of playing in the pros are high. What the waterboy's wish of dealing with sports science can turn an athlete into a super athlete. Not to mention curing the pains that some dealt with in the last twenty years in sports. I had friends who retired early because of injuries and concussions. I do believe I've seen the future version of me, if they don't make the same mistakes that I've done.

***

A few hours later, I went back to my house, and I worry about my little brother. I thought what if his cure for cancer would turn into a complete failure. My brother would be completely devastated if his facts are not as accurate as he thought it would be. I hope the thought of my brother's engagement does not hurt the opportunity. Without warning, I heard a knock on the door. I'm thinking it was Tim wanted to talk to me. As I open the door, I didn't expect her to show up.

"Is it okay to come in?"

It was Lisa, I don't know how she found me. I invited her over to have a talk.

"First of all, I want to apologize for my behavior last night."

"I accept your apology, Jeff. I also want to apologize for my actions last night. My behavior was inappropriate."

"There's no need to apologize, Lisa. My brother was right, I am a jerk."

Without warning, she kissed me. I was completely shocked.

"Lisa! What were you thinking!"

"I can't help it, I'm intrigued about you when I first saw you."

"I thought you're interested in my brother's research. Better still, I thought you love Tim."

Lisa laughed at my response. I began to notice something.

"Do you think I'm interested in your brother?"

"I thought that he would be in love with you."

Lisa continued laughing at being in love with Tim.

"He cares more about his stupid research than he ever cares about me."

Poor Tim, if I told him Lisa took advantage of him, he would be in total denial. I'll never forgive myself to tell Tim the truth.

"Look, I don't want to be the one who'd destroy a partnership, but Tim loves you."

"Jeff, your brother is a fool. Do you think I partnered with him to create a cure to benefit mankind?"

"How many people died from that plague?"

"I don't care about the ones who suffer from the disease. I care about making a profit from the highest bidder."

"You witch! You sold him out for no reason."

"Why do you care about him? It's not like you don't love him to begin with, you has-been."

"That was out of line, I hated my brother because he was different. As I got older, he tries to help people who are more important than he is. Yes, I was jealous of him as a kid. Yes, I was jealous of him as an adult. However I am proud of my brother. I am the one who is mad at myself. I'm calling him and tell him what's going on!"

But as I grab the phone to call Tim. I got hit in the back of my head, rendering me unconscious. The next thing I knew, I woke up and saw my brother dead with the gun that I kept in the safe on the floor. That's when your colleagues place me under arrest for the murder of Dr. Timothy Hagen.

***

"That's all I could remember."

Jeff drank his coffee as the detectives listen. Detective Grendel gave Jeff a surprised compliment.

"I'm surprised you're calm after all the misery you went through."

"I deserve to get yelled at, but your partner played the role of peacemaker as I talked."

Grendel looked to his partner and asked him why he was so calm for the last hour and a half. The rookie partner had one simple explanation.

"Faith, Leon. It's called having faith, especially when it comes to those who fall short."

"Where do you learn that?"

Jeff tells Grendel how his partner learned. "The Bible, your partner is more to that."

"He has to; he has a brother who preaches on Sundays."

Malloy asked the suspect one more question. "Jeff, do you know where Dr. Van Janssen is?"

"No, my guess is she must've run when she heard the gunshot."

Out of the blue, Officer Abernathy opened the door telling Jeff and the detectives bad news.

"I got some info about Dr. Van Janssen as Malloy requested. I found out that she's not who she is."

Grendel becomes suspicious. "What do you mean, she's not?"

"Dr. Van Janssen is a spy for a rival lab. There's also a report that somebody broke into Dr. Hagen's lab."

Jeff knows what Lisa is looking for. "She might be looking for my brother's cure. If she finds it, his work will go down the toilet."

Grendel tells his partner a simple task. "Jim, take Hagen back to his cell, then come with me to the lab."

Jeff wants to help. "I want to go, detectives. Tim's legacy is not going to be in vain if we stop Lisa immediately."

Grendel thought about what Jeff said, and decides what was best for the case.

"I'm going against my judgement, but you're right. You're coming with us."

Jim smiled, "You're ready for this, Jeff."

"I'm ready to make things right for my brother."

Grendel had one thing to say. "Let's roll."

Jeff and the detectives head out the door and drove off to Tim's office at Hagen Labs. From there, Lisa was inside ransacking his office looking for the formula.

Where is it, she thought as she tossed the files like it was nothing but trash. Without warning, there was a knock on the door. Lisa thought that it was the custodian. She kept on looking for the file until the police bust the door down. Grendel pointed his gun at Lisa.

"FREEZE! You're under arrest!"

"NO! You can't arrest me. I have done nothing wrong!"

Jeff disagreed. "I beg to differ, you killed my brother."

"It was foolproof. I know that you hated Tim for everything he's accomplished. But what he did was selfish."

Malloy took out the handcuffs. "What would that be Miss Van Janssen, trying to find a cure for cancer?"

"No, it's selling the formula to the highest pharmaceutical. When Tim found out I tried to sell the cure, he fired me."

Jeff knew his feelings of Lisa were true. "I always knew you were trouble the moment I saw you. Even though I was mean to my brother, I protected him. You were somebody I thought he would love."

"Instead, I wanted more than love. I wanted somebody with a large bank account. That's why I unlocked the gun safe and took out your gun to kill him, to blame you."

Lisa's response brought her to tears as she drops the last file on the ground, and got on her knees. Malloy slapped on the handcuffs as he read Lisa her rights. Jeff looked at the file, which had the notes from Tim's research. He notices that the cure for cancer that Tim was creating was a total failure. Jeff knew that Tim was completely devastated with the results.

Detective Grendel looked at Jeff down at what he's been feeling.

"I thought you would be happy that we caught your brother's killer."

Jeff looked at the veteran detective and was sad. "There's no way I can be happy with what's going on."

"C'mon, let me give you a ride home."

The two men left the trashed office together. Jeff Hagen's jealousy of his brother caused him to be grief stricken because of his death. He called his father with the horrible news and felt he was responsible for Tim's death. His father said that Jeff wasn't responsible. He explained even though he and his mom treated Jeff unlike his brother. They still love him like any parent would when somebody has two or more children. Jeff prayed to God asking him for forgiveness of his jealousy that he had on Tim. After he prayed, Jeff lay down on his bed, crying.

***

The next morning, Jeff got a call from Detective Malloy asking him to come down to the station. As he got there, he saw a box of stuff from Tim's office including a flash drive and a letter from Tim directed to Jeff. Jeff reads the whole letter with specific instructions with what was on the drive. Tim's life work on the cure for cancer. He didn't want the cure to fall into anybody's greedy hands, which is why he created decoys on the files. Tim knew the flash drive that Jeff held onto would carry on his life's work. Malloy wondered where Tim's files will go.

"Where would this go to?"

"The college has a medical center. I hope and pray the scientists there could finish what Tim has started."

Grendel thought there wasn't a cure. "I thought the cure for cancer was only a theory."

"You don't know my brother like I do, detective. Once he has something on his mind, he sticks to it."

Malloy picked up the phone. "I'll contact the college."

Jeff placed the stick and Tim's instructions on an envelope to the medical center. As he seals the envelope, Jeff Hagen has one thing on his mind.

"This time Tim, you will find a cure."

Jealousy is a type of hatred that is more like going one-up on somebody. For Jeff Hagen, his rivalry with his late brother show only despair. He accepted the fact that what we do is more important than what accolades or possessions we have. Everyone has a unique gift and what we do with that gift is up to us. The two brothers in the end became co-MVPs of the game that counts; the game known as life.

Sin #7 PRIDE

Here we are, boys & girls; we're down to the final sin. And to all Christians, we place this sin as the top of our list. Why is the deadliest of all the seven deadly sins? Because this sin makes us think of nobody else but ourselves. Think of it this way, what happens when the person you love decided to leave you? Or what would happen if you make all the money in the world, and it goes as it comes? What happen when all you have left in the world is your own selfish pride?

Pride is a desire to love one's own self. Caring about nobody but you, or blaming everybody but you could be your personal downfall. Because this sin causes cockiness, arrogance, and even vanity. I know some people who say they're better than anybody, but they're nothing but fools. In order for you to accept Jesus as your Lord and Savior, you need to be more humble. That means you get on your knees, bow down your head, and confess you're a sinner asking for forgiveness. Sometimes, a good cry doesn't hurt either. Somebody should tell the person in my next story this little lesson. Because it's about a model who is more like the ultimate diva. I call this tale of vanity:

CATWALK

Catwalk
A Tale of Pride

N ew York City, for millions of people, it's the greatest city in the world. Every year, it's the place for the biggest week for clothing designers. It's Fashion Week, and almost everybody gathers for the annual event. The new looks could be the difference between what will sell in department stores. And what disasters could get arrested by the Fashion Police.

Fashion Week kicked off with the new collection from Antoine. The models prepare to walk on the catwalk, but there was one little problem. The main model for this campaign is late, which made fashion designer Antoine Morgan upset.

"Where is she? She could be stuck in traffic, or worse. She could be with one of her new boy toys from those tacky tabloids."

All of a sudden, his star arrived from the back door. It was Heather McDougal, the mega hot supermodel. Heather gave Antoine air kisses while Antoine gave her a lot of grief.

"Where have you been? I've already started my show, and you hang around with your new boy toy."

"I'm here, am I? Don't try to be too upset."

Heather brought her emergency make-up and hairstyling team with her at all times. Antoine continued to be a nervous wreck.

"Will you hurry up; I'm going to be a laughing stock!"

Heather's hairstylist looks at Antoine. "Beauty like hers takes time. I recommend you should use a little less eyeliner."

After a quick makeover, and a change of clothes, Heather is ready to go. The cameras are on her like a colony of ants to the annual company picnic. The crowd saw Heather walked down the runway like she was the queen. Antoine's fashion show became a success, but Antoine isn't happy with Heather's tardiness. After the show, Heather talked with entertainment reporters about the show. She talked more about herself. A lone reporter saw Antoine all alone. He asked Antoine about Heather. Antoine told him what he thought about his star model behind closed doors.

***

A few hours later, Heather goes to a big fashion party. As she heads to the elevator, a group of teenagers asked her for her autograph. Heather walked away from her young fans as the elevator door starts closing. This made her young fans disappointed. The elevator moved up to the penthouse floor, and the door opens for Heather as she heads to the fashion party. Anybody who is anybody was there, and Heather was likely to be anywhere. Unbeknownst to Heather, a few people watched TV and saw Antoine's interview. Everyone listened to what the fashion designer thought of Heather. Heather was too busy trying to get a glass of champagne.

"My star model is nothing but trouble. She's always late, and cares about nobody but herself."

Heather turned around hearing more of the interview. By what she heard, she became furious.

The interviewer had one more question to ask Antoine. "Will she do another runway show for you again, Antoine?"

Antoine gave the interviewer his answer. "As of now, she'll never do another runway show for me. She is what you guys called, 'fired!'"

Everybody is in shock to hear about Antoine's firing of Heather. Heather became furious. As Antoine arrived, she took a glass of champagne and splashed it right into Antoine's face. Heather left the party crying as the elevator goes down. As she headed to the limousine for home; Heather McDougal thought that with the first day being over, she doesn't need Antoine. She believed any designer would have her model for their show.

***

The following day, everybody talked about the fashion show, and the disastrous post-show party. Heather's assault on Antoine was also top news fodder. Antoine went on a talk show talking about the embarrassing moments. Not to mention what happened at the after party. Meanwhile, Heather was the last to know about these things. She slept at her lavish $8 million dollar apartment. The phone rang, it was her agent Travis, and he wasn't in a happy mood. He told Heather that after the fiasco, no other fashion show would have her on. And no designer would call her. Heather got so mad, she hanged up the phone. She turned on the TV, and saw continuous coverage of her fall from grace. She cried on her expensive couch she bought from Italy. She knew what she did last night is now target fodder for entertainment news shows. All a sudden, the phone rang again. Heather was crying up an ocean, so she let the answering machine get it.

The answering machine played this message. "Hi, this is Heather. I'm not here because I'm having a fabulous time somewhere. If you leave your name & message after the beep, I'll call you back and we'll talk about my favorite subject, ME!"

After the beep, a stranger wanted to talk to Heather later today at Chez Chuy, alone.

***

A few hours later, Heather went incognito at Chez Chuy hoping nobody noticed her. She sat at the table alone for her mysterious benefactor to show up. Out of the blue, a man comes up to Heather's table.

"Excuse me, ma'am, is this seat taken?"

Heather gave the mystery man her answer. "I'm waiting for somebody who called me earlier today."

"That would be me. I'm the one who called you today."

121

"Well, in that case, please have a seat. I'll ask the waiter for some wine."

After Heather's new admirer sat down, the two started to talk business. Heather asked the hard questions.

"The first question I want to ask you is; who are you, and what do you want with me?"

"Actually, you told me two questions. I'll answer them both for you. My name is Gordy Lambert, and I'm a fashion designer."

Heather becomes disappointed, she wasn't sure if any fashion designer would hire her. With the news of her blacklisted from every fashion show, she might be in the mood for a miracle.

"Why do you want to talk to me? I mean nobody from the fashion world would ever talk to me since..."

Gordy interrupted what Heather would say. "Since you splashed Antoine with a glass of vintage 1952 Dom Perignon."

"How did you know that?"

"Well, I always knew Dom Perignon gets better with age. Also, my mother ran a vineyard when I was little."

"Paris?"

"No, Fresno."

Heather & Gordy laughed at his comment. However, Heather wondered why Gordy wants her. Is he one of those tabloid reporters, or somebody who wants her back in the spotlight. Heather knows that Gordy hasn't answered her other question.

"As for your second question, I'm here to help you get back on the runway. I'm a firm believer of second chances."

"Well, it's too late for that."

"Not true. I have a runway show coming this Friday, and I want you to be part of it."

"Are you kidding me!"

The people told Heather to quiet down.

"Gordy took out his business card. "Give me a call if you're interested."

Heather couldn't believe what happened. Somebody gave her a second chance. But Heather wondered if Gordy was there to help her, or is it another attack on her own pride.

After the dinner, Heather headed back to her lavish apartment. She turned on the TV, and there was more bad news about her. Designers & models have each expressed their opinions about her, the opinions are negative. As she hears more bad news, Heather looked at the business card she got, and knew exactly what to do. She dialed up the number hoping that Gordy would answer the phone. The phone started to rang on the other end, and a certain voice answers the phone.

"Hello."

"Is this Gordy?"

"That would be me, Heather. How are you doing?"

"I'm doing okay, even though they treat me like trash."

"Don't pay any attention to those fools, Heather. When you return to the runway, you'll be the one having the last laugh. Then they'll be sorry."

Heather chuckled with what her new admirer had to say. If there's anybody who want to help her it would be Gordy Lambert.

"I wondered if you would come to my studio tomorrow at 2:00."

"I can be there at 2:00."

"I run a tight ship, and I don't like it when people are late."

"I promise you, I will not be late. I'll be there on time."

"I'll see you then, Heather. Bye-bye."

"Bye, Gordy. Thank you for everything."

As Heather hanged up the phone, she squealed with delight. It's her way of telling the fashion industry to take their blacklists where the sun never shines. Heather as good luck would have it headed off to bed as she dreams about being back where she belongs; on top.

***

The next day, Heather McDougal arrived at Gordy's designer studio. What's more amazing is that she arrived fifteen minutes earlier. Gordy is very surprised.

"I am pleased to see you. I never thought you would arrive this early."

"Let's say I changed my wicked ways since Monday. I'm ready to make a brand new start."

Gordy was happy to see that. "That's what I like to hear. I'm glad to see you're planning to turn your life around."

"So, what will I model for your collection?"

"I haven't made a decision with what you'll wear for the show."

"Is it going to be a surprise?"

"Let's say that when you work the runway," Gordy replied. "You'll knock them dead."

Heather smiled at Gordy's remark. She dreamed that she was walking the runway with Gordy's newest fashion design. And saw everybody who gave her the harsh news and negative publicity dropped dead. Gordy tries to bring Heather back to reality.

"Heather... Heather... Heather!"

Heather snapped out of her daydream.

"Huh? Did you say something?"

"I asked if you want a glass of champagne. I wanted to celebrate our new business relationship."

"Oh, that," she chuckled in confusion. "I'd love to have a glass of champagne."

Gordy brings out a bottle of champagne. He tells Heather that this is a special bottle he was going to save for the end of Friday's show. However, he thinks that today is a special event.

"Heather, I'd like to propose a toast. Here's to another shot at being back on top."

Heather has her own toast in mind. "I'd like to propose a toast, too. Here is to a start of a brand new relationship, business wise of course."

"Of course, this is a business relationship."

As the glasses clang, Heather sipped her champagne. She never tried champagne that had such a kick. Heather almost fell, but Gordy was there to catch her.

"Whoa, Gordy, where did you get the grapes for this champagne? I mean this is very strong stuff."

"This is a special kind of champagne. My mom gave this to me all the way from Fresno."

"France has got nothing on this wine."

"That's because it's not from France. Fresno is in California. I told you my mom ran a vineyard when I was a kid. When I first moved to New York, she gave me a case of her special wine."

"Your mom must be somebody special."

"She is. My father is a different story."

"Why is that? Did you have an argument when you left Fresno?"

"I didn't have an argument with him. When I was a teenager, my father died of a heart attack. I wanted to tell him that I wanted to move to New York. But as I was going to tell him, I saw him dead next to the truck. He was loading the crates of grapes to the truck."

"I'm sorry, Gordy. My father never cared much for me anyway. In fact, he kicked me & my mother out of my house when I was thirteen."

"Was your father abusive?"

"Yes, he abused my mother when he drinks. He drank malt liquor or cognac."

"Did you deal with the pain of divorce?"

"No, she filed for divorce. Before she left my father, he killed my mother in cold blood. He was serving life in prison. He died three years ago."

"Who raised you after your parents died?"

"My grandmother, she was the strictest person I know. She takes me to church every Sunday morning since I first moved there. She was also a great teacher and mentor. I didn't go to the funeral when she died two years ago. For the first time in my life, I'm all alone."

Gordy felt Heather's pain, he thought it was best for her to go home and call it a day.

***

The next day, with the show a mere twenty-four hours away. The press is having a field day with Gordy Lambert's upcoming fashion show. And what's even more shocking is that he brought Heather McDougal in to be in the show. Every reporter wanted to ask Gordy why he is risking the chance to work with Heather. Gordy answers every reporter's question like he's coated in Teflon.

"I admit the risk that I'm working with Ms. McDougal. I knew about her diva past, but I'm here to tell you she's got what most divas haven't gotten, a second chance."

A reporter had a question for Heather.

"Why has Mr. Lambert gave you a second chance?"

Heather gave her answer. "For the last six years I wanted to be the best supermodel. However, I acted more like a diva, and less like a human being. I hanged around with A-listers, but after what Antoine said on Monday's show was true. I was selfish, spoiled, and completely egotistical. Gordy has done what others wouldn't do, and that is giving me faith to come back and model once again."

After the press conference, Gordy & Heather celebrated. The two got into the limousine and headed to a place that Heather has never been to, Gordy's apartment. The limo stopped at the door and Heather & Gordy headed straight to the penthouse. The two giggled like a couple of schoolchildren as they head to Gordy's apartment door. As they entered, Heather stood in amazement at what the apartment looks like. The furniture in his living room came from Paris. The handcrafted dining room table came from Italy. His bookshelf has works from Shakespeare, Homer, and Dickens. Heather thought to herself that her new boss is more than what he appears to be.

"Wow! I'm impressed with what you've done to this place. This must've cost you a fortune."

"It cost a lot to live here, but it doesn't hurt to have some help."

"Did you have somebody help you find this place?"

"Actually this place was my mother's old apartment. She gave me the keys to this place when I went to NYU."

"You went to school at NYU? I thought you go out and party with all those snooty types."

Gordy wasn't the partying type. "No, I go to school and head home when I first moved here. I'm not a party person."

Heather couldn't believe it. "You're kidding. You live in the greatest city in the world, and you don't go to parties like the ones during Fashion Week."

"I'm a homebody. Every time I go to a party, I'm the odd one out."

Heather is in shock to hear what Gordy said. Gordy wanted to eat dinner before it gets cold. He asked Heather to head to the dining room table while he gets a bottle of wine. Heather sat down to look at the pictures surrounding the dining room. The paintings gave Heather the creeps as Gordy brought the wine.

"Where did you get the paintings?"

"Those paintings are my creations. I wanted to be an artist when I first moved here. My parents were not amused at first, but I like them."

"They look like they're from a bad horror film. I'm scared of horror films."

Gordy seemed a little sad. He loves Heather, but he doesn't want to frighten her away. Out of the blue, he had an idea to make Heather safe and happy.

"How about we eat by the fireplace?"

Heather got concerned. "Is there any more of those creepy paintings there?"

"No, not at all. I need to renovate the dining room anyway."

The two started enjoying their dinner in front of the fireplace. The blaze of a warm fire made the room feel more romantic. Heather asked Gordy what her motivation would be for tomorrow's show. Gordy looks at her big brown eyes and said in one sly reply.

"Tomorrow, you're going to make them remember you."

"I love what you said."

After dinner, Heather knew it was getting late, and Gordy called up the limo to take her home. Heather gives Gordy a kiss as she gets a little sleepy knowing that tomorrow will be a big day. Gordy looks down and smiled knowing that Heather will be big news without even knowing it.

***

Friday, the big day. For Heather McDougal, it is a day for redemption. A day that she goes from riches to rags and back to riches again. Heather turned on the TV to find any more news about her return to the modeling world. However, there was nothing said about her or Gordy's upcoming fashion show tonight. At first she thought it was early, but she got nervous with the show fast approaching. Without warning, the phone starts ringing, and Heather picked it up.

"Hello. Oh, hi Gordy! Yes, I'm watching the TV. I wanted to know why hasn't there been any news about tonight's fashion show?"

Gordy told Heather that his show is top secret for tonight. And what Gordy has in mind for tonight's show is going to make every designer jealous. Heather likes what Gordy said, but she has one more question to ask him.

"What time do you want me to be there?"

Gordy replied over the phone that she needed to be at the show at 6:00 PM.

"I'll be there. I'll see you tonight, Gordy. Bye-bye."

Heather hanged up the phone and thought about the last few days as a nightmare. With her comeback a few hours away, she knows all the bad press she suffered will end. For Heather McDougal, it's time for her to get the last word.

***

A few hours later, Heather McDougal arrived at Gordy's fashion show. Gordy is happy to see that she arrived a half hour earlier than he expected. Gordy knows Heather is punctual.

"Wow! I never expect you to come here this early, Heather."

"Like you told me before, If I'm going to work for somebody like you, I need to change my wicked ways for good."

"That's the way I like about you. The rest of the models won't arrive for another hour. I brought some of my best champagnes here after the show. But this, I only wanted to share this with you."

After Gordy popped the cork, he poured the special bubbly over the glasses. Heather couldn't help but to ask Gordy a question.

"Why are we drinking this early?"

"Because this bottle is for the two of us. This is your special comeback, and I wanted to celebrate this with you and nobody else."

"That makes sense."

Heather picked up her glass as Gordy prepares a toast.

"Here's to you and your big comeback."

"I'll drink to that."

The two clanged their glasses together, and Heather sips her champagne. Gordy couldn't help but to look at Heather and smile.

Heather liked the taste of the champagne. "This is good champagne. What do you call this?"

"This is a special brand that I made. It's called, 'la baiser de la mort.'"

"It sounds romantic. What does it mean?"

Gordy looked at Heather with a wicked smile. "It's French for, 'The kiss of death.'"

Heather laughed. "Why do you call it the kiss of death?"

"I made this champagne with a hint of nightshade."

"Are you saying that what I'm drinking is..."

Before she says another word, Heather begins to choke.

"That's right, Heather. It's made of poison. You're dead."

Heather's voice turned weak from the poison. "What did I ever do to you?"

Gordy explained why he did it. "Nothing. It's what you done to my partner, Antoine."

Heather McDougal has gone from one of the top supermodels in the world to a victim of a cruel twist of fate. Gordy now has a new problem, what to do with the body of a dead supermodel. He takes the body out back and gets her ready for his nightmarish creation. Moments later, some of the other models came in as the show starts.

***

8:00 PM, magic time. Everybody in the modeling world was there. Even Antoine showed up to see Heather's big comeback. The lights are on, and the background was the sight of a graveyard, promoting the new line Gory by Gordy. Models dressed in fashion that looks like it came out of the morgue. Most of the crowd is in shock to see these new designs. They were even more shocked to see Heather McDougal walking down the runway. The audience didn't suspect her held by invisible wires like a puppet. People applauded the success of Gordy's fashion show. They were also pleased with Heather's return to modeling, but her return was short-lived.

129

After the show, Gordy disposed Heather's body as Antoine congratulated his partner's show.

"I got to hand it to you, Gordy. You look like you've got away with murder."

Gordy laughed and smile at Antoine's response. I did. My assistant is bringing us some champagne. Would you like some?"

"Yes, please."

As the two designers started celebrating, the assistant asked his boss a question.

"What is the name on the bottle? All I can read is 'la basier de la mort'."

Antoine started to choke. "Where did you get that champagne?"

"I found it in the back. I knew somebody drank some of it when I pour the glasses."

Antoine & Gordy were victims of their own foul play. They never suspect they each took a sip of the champagne known as 'la basier de la mort', the kiss of death. And the two top designers drop dead from their own brand of sweet revenge. It was their pride to commit the perfect murder of Heather McDougal. The police found the body two days later at the alley near Gordy's studio.

Heather McDougal was once the top diva in the modeling world until her own selfish pride caught up with her. She should've learn more to think of others and a little less of herself. It's a lesson we all need to remind ourselves every once in a while.

Afterward

Ladies and Gentlemen, we've now concluded our little field trip of our seven sinful tales. I hope that you've paid attention with these traps against morality and honesty.

Now that the tour has ended, I want to ask you a few questions:

Do you spend most of your time in bars pursuing sins of the flesh?

Are you more of a scrooge?

Do you ever do something mean to somebody you are now regretting later?

Are you jealous of someone who's doing better than you?

If you answered yes to any of these questions, ask yourself the big question. If you die tomorrow, are you 100% sure that you're going to heaven?

A couple years ago, a preacher asked me the same question, and he helped me get saved. I'm going to do the same for you, use this simple prayer:

Dear God:

I am praying to you because I have sinned. I have come to ask you to save me from all the despair and turmoil of all my sins. And I want to accept Jesus Christ as my lord and savior because he died for my sins. I will change my wicked and sinful ways in Jesus' name I pray. AMEN.

If you say this simple prayer, you've taken the first step forward to salvation. If you don't know how to accept, ask your love ones or your pastor, they can help too. Remember in John 8:12, Jesus said the he is the light of the world, and if you follow him you won't be walking in darkness, but you'll have the light of life. And with this country being sick from drugs, lust, greed and corruption, we need a savior to light our way.

Thank you for reading and taking the first step forward; good luck, and God bless you.

www.ingramcontent.com/pod-product-compliance
Lightning Source LLC
Chambersburg PA
CBHW030534130626
46552CB00006B/2258